NEW VISION
PUBLICATION
PRESENTS

still Damaged

The Coldest Bitch Ever...

PART

A NOVEL BY

LSD GONZALEZ

ISBN: (13) 978-0-9836039-2-4
Cover design: www.mariondesigns.com
Inside layout: www.mariondesigns.com
Typist and Typset: Linda Williams

Still Damaged a novel/LSD Gonzales

P.O. Box 2815
Stockbridge, GA 30281
www.newvisionpublication.com

First Printing July 2011
Printed in Canada

10   9   8   7   6   5   4   3   2   1

This one is for you old head

"Ishmael Bonnie Helms"

R.I.P.

DEDICATION

This book is dedicated; to the three Queens who stood by me side when everybody else abandoned me. Maria Gonzalez, Rafaila Santiago, and Anna Rondon. Mami Anna, thank you for all the love you give me. If I would've listened to your advice, I probably wouldn't be here today. Titi Rafi, you always treated me as your son-I miss you.

Mom, no matter how much time pass, you will live in my heart forever. Knowing you are watching my back at all times, gives me the strength to face adversities with a sense of dignity. I miss you like hell mom. You never got to see my first book in print, but trust me; all your inputs are up in there. (R.I.P)

ACKNOWLEDGMENTS

All praise is due to God. Without Him none of this would have been possible.

Now, I'd like to start by thanking Linda Williams. My friend, partner, mentor, mother in this game, what would I do without you in my life? From day one you kept it one hundred with me. Even when the industry politics tried to do me dirty, you stood by my side and made it happen for me. Thank you for everything you done for me. Thank you for the books, the money orders, accepting my collect calls, the letters, and for the guidance you have given me throughout this rough journey. Your realness has shown me that even in this dirty dog world, the publishing biz, there are still a few honorable people who respect real. Trust me, we will land on the best sellers list.

To the head man of New Vision and my New Vision family. Words can't express my sincere appreciation for the opportunity you have given me to bring some real fire to the streets from a Puerto Rican perspective. It's unheard of in this business to submit a manuscript for consideration in August, and have it publish by November. That shows the level of dedication that New Vision has for their writers. I'm hoping this relationship sets the stage for bigger and better things for us. If you thought *Damaged: The Diary of A Lost Soul* was hot, then part 2, *Still Damaged: The Coldest Bitch* ever is sizzling! The streets need us!

I've been label *The demon of The Black Ink*, because of my raw, in your face, style of writing. Let me be clear, I write for the streets and the true hard core, urban fiction heads who appreciate real.

To the bookstores: Empire Books, Black Visions Books, Hood Books Headquarters, Horizon Book Store, Nubian Book Store and Black And Novel Book Store, thanks for all the love.

To all people who bought Damage, "Thank you."

To RC and family. Y'all the best. Throughout my trials and tribulation you been there for me as a real friend. Soon the world would know who RC, Attorney at Law is.

To my main crew: Fed, Ray-Ray Lopez and family, Fox Zafir, Caz, Ike, Magic, Mojica, Jose, Billy, Polo, Fifi, Ali, Ol' head Frank Ross, Roger, Gerry, Spade, Spil, Ed, Julia Lopez, Luis Sanabria, J.D., Amanda Winky, Ruth Kull, Van, Judith Trustone E.S.L Mike K, Rocky, Chalie-Block, Run, Chuck, Tommy, Ray Yabor, Map, Sun, Angelita Rodriguez, John Griffin, Dee, Lil' Shari, Big Shrif, Kabasha, Coke, Lolo, Cuba! Listen here; you have the skills to be one of the best in this game. Your time to shine will come. YaYa, I love you like a brother. I can't wait until you drop your book. Trust me, *Get Snitch Face* will be a smash! To Neno Mosantos, let's get this money together.

To my sisters and brothers, and family, Julie, Eva, Annie Damarie, Tambo, Milagro, David, Tony, Jennifer, Jenny and Melvan, even though from time to time y'all forget y'all got a brother lock up, I still got love for y'all. To all the little ones who look up to me, Niki, Anajay, Maria, Kimberly, Chuchi, Elizabeth, Kathy, Jennifer, Jonathan, Jusha, Lil' Dave, and Jacob.

To Ray Pastrana and family. Ol' head you are the closest thing I have to a big brother, the most honorable man in the world, I really appreciate everything you have done for me. Not too many people keep their word, once they bounce from this place.

To Maria Hinojosa and family, thank you for all the support throughout the years. You are a real friend.

To Joy/Deja King, you inspired me to go hard on my writing.

Your work has shown me how to bring fire to the readers. Thanks for all your books!

To all the haters, Damn! I'm dropping book after book and y'all still wondering how I'm doing it, I know y'all be coping this book, that's the only way y'all going to be able to read it! Maybe some of y'all haters may become fans.

Puerto Rico! Stand up! I'm representing that Boricua arroz con gandules y pollo azado flow.

To all those who been trying to reach out to me. You could send all letters/comments and/or questions you may have to: Luis S. Gonzalez, AS-0834, P.O. Box 244, Collegeville, PA 19426.

Finally, shout out to the streets! Y'all determine who gonna shine next in this book game. My name was called and I answered, with the Realest Book the streets will ever read. *Still Damaged: The Coldest Bitch Ever.*

LSD Gonzalez
The Demon of The Black Ink

"And ye shall know the Truth
and the Truth shall set ye free"

PROLOGUE

Philadelphia...

The urge to leave my present life behind was overwhelming. After all, I had enough money and resources to reinvest myself in another city.

In my life there's no room for any regrets, therefore I haven't lost any sleep since sending Sweep Lip's and Cuba to their permanent destination. They were nothing to me except two pieces of shit who thought they could cross me. Yeah! I know you're probably thinking I'm a rotten bitch-you're right, you have no idea how rotten I can be.

I am what I am, and until the end I will always be the coldest bitch ever. Fuck with me and there will be hell to pay, I have no problem administrating justice my way.

Being an CIA agent is something serious, depending on who you ask. Personally, I love it because it allows me to destroy all the maggots and roaches running around fucking little kids in the ass. By no means am I referring to your typical, next door child molester. I'm talking about men of power in high places. Free mason, Senators, judges, city cops and yes, even CIA agents. These muthafuckas are the same assholes who sit's in the comfort of a luxury office unloading kiddy pornography onto government computers using tax dollars to travel the third world countries such as Brazil, Thailand, and Colombia to fulfill their fantasy by fucking babies, then they come back to U.S. soil wanting to implement they brand of morality on people like me. Fuck them all, I have no loyalty to such perverts.

Our justice system is rooted on corruption and these assholes who call the shots, don't give a fuck about our kids. They will lie and cover up for each other. Don't be fooled by their appearance. Behind close doors in the hallways of Capital Hill, sit some of the nation most notorious babies' rapist.

On the surface my mission in Philadelphia seemed completed. I could, easily disappear from the city of brotherly Love without a trace, but why should I? I have every intention of penetrating the lives of these high ranking assholes.

My action invertebrately threatens the well-being of some and the reputation of others. I intend to expose a hidden connection between your respectable Senator, Mayor and the thug out nigga on the block. Yes, even if you don't see these sick muthafuckas in the hood, they are there via money-hungry sick bastards who specialize in destroying the lives of innocent kids.

I could speak on this shit with a sense of authority

because I've been there. I'm a product of the foster care system. I've been fuck in the ass, by my foster care father. All my life, I've been physically and sexually abuse by men in high places, so I'm bound to these assholes by a secret so ruthless, that it will destroy the way the average person view their government officials.

In the course of me exposing these assholes many people will find themselves in some fuck up predicaments, some may even die, but who gives a fuck? In order for justice to be served there can be no compromising on the fundamental requirement: the truth and nothing but the truth.

I'm opening the files related to kiddy pornography scandal within the government in the city of Brotherly Love. Whoever don't like it, can kiss my Puerto Rican fat ass. If you thought Watergate was big, wait until I unleash "Government officials fucking kids' scandals."

CIA Headquarters...

The main office for the Central Intelligence Agency, CIA is located in Langley, Virginia, about seven to eight miles from Washington, DC. The building is heavily guarded twenty-four seven, and only authorized agents are allowed to enter. Inside the corridor and above the main entrance a verse is carved on the wall which read:

"And ye shall know the Truth
and the Truth shall set ye free"

This is a place where not too many muthafuckas from the hood would ever set foot.

In the first floor conference room, guarded armed white men with Glock 9s under their blue suites stood outside the conference room with strict order, shoot first and ask questions later, if any unauthorized personnel attempts to enter the conference room.

A week after ATF agent Ed "Cuba" Sanchez was assassinated down in Philadelphia, an executive staff meeting was under way. Seated around a large table were a bunch of high ranking CIA officials who were supposed to be in charge of our national security. Peter Newman, a CIA agent who is the intelligence point man officer in the East Cost. Sidney Weldon, CIA Director, and Chief of Counterintelligence, Ted Connors. Ted was the only black, well, half black-Dominican in the meeting. He was a stubborn, Uncle Tom asshole! He owned a chain of Day Care Center around the country, and was wealthy. He had gone through five out of control marriages. His last wife accused him of sexually abusing his twelve year old daughter, but her accusation was squashed before she even had a chance to tell her story to federal prosecutors. Ted used all his resources to silence her. She mysteriously was murdered one day while she went out for her daily run in the park.

"Fellows, today we are meeting here because someone within our branch is tapping into our personal computers.

This meeting today is off the records-no records will be kept and everyone will be addressed by their first name only," Ted said, paranoia blossoming inside his head. The disturbing information he had gather from Philadelphia could send the structure he build crumbling to the ground, and he could land somewhere in the maximum-security prison in Florence, Colorado a place he help build.

Everyone seating around the oak table shook their heads, Ted continued, "I have received some disturbing information. My contact in Philadelphia, are reporting back to me that some of our associates have been indicted on child sex abuse and one has been murder in his chamber. I've been told that Larry McCall had to be eliminated. I've also been asked to keep this information in the strictest of confidentially. But it's only fair that I share it with you all, because any scandal involving any of our associates would reflect badly on us, the CIA." There was a look of total disbelief on Sidney face.

"How do we make this mess in Philadelphia disappear? I'm not trying to be a cell-mate with Ted Kaczynski, the Unabomber," Sidney asked.

"I pretty much took care of everything, so be patient, buddy," Ted responded.

"Good! Than we all can relax, right?" Peter said in a low tone of voice.

"No! We can never relax. We need to be more careful of how we conduct our business," Ted said. For the next few seconds, everyone seating around the table looked at each other back and forth.

It was Friday, and every Friday night Sidney and a group of good ole boys would participate in kinky sex with underage boys. The only one in the CIA office, who knew this, was the ones seating in the room. They all shared the same dark secret.

Ted probably was the freakiest one of the group. He loved to be tie up and raped by young men, mostly Hispanic males from the projects in DC, until his blood flowed out his asshole, each time he would cry out like a bitch "I am a bad boy! Oh God, I love this." After every session these freaky perverts would pay the young men top dollars for their service. The flip side of this sick game was that Ted had career ambitions and wouldn't hesitate crossing any of the man in the room.

"This one significant incident down in Philadelphia will influence the way we conduct business in the months to come," Ted looked everyone in the eyes. *I hope these assholes don't make me turn this into a matter of life and death.*

"Enjoy your weekend."

Three Years Before...

I was recruited right in college by an ethic teacher

who wanted to get into my panties.

I sat in front of his desk with my skirt up high giving him a good view of my pussy. He adjusted his glasses and looked at me

"What can I help you with young lady?" he asked, staring directly between my legs.

"I just wanted to know what this ethic class consisted of. And can I take it as a free elective?"

Shit! This young bitch got a beautiful pussy. Danmit! She got me coming on myself. Thank God I'm not circumcised, if not I'd be leaking all over the place.

"Young lady, this class consist of ethics in intelligence work. It's a mandated class for all students interested in law enforcement, and yes you can take it as a free elective," Dr. Harvey Connors said, still staring at my pussy.

"Listen Dr. Connors, lets save my time and yours, and just tell me what's the price is going to be for a passing grade if I register for your class?" Dr. Connor was struck by my blunt remark, but I could see his hard on. His eyes were buzzing, with lustful thoughts

"Young lady, I'm very much respected in this university. At this moment, even having this conversation with you makes me very uncomfortable," he responded trying to hide his hard on by placing a note book on top of his lap. Rumors around Temple University, amongst students were that Dr. Connors would generously give out passing grades to anyone willing to satisfy his freaky desires, such as urinating in his mouth, and I be damn, if I wasn't going to get in his class and get a passing grade.

"Dr. Connors, there's an exception for everything." He tried to remain calm, but the sight of some young pussy staring him in the face had him wound up inside. His dick was harder than an aluminum bat. Plotting his next move, he got up and closed the door, securing it from the inside.

I know this is unethical, but I just want to taste that young pussy.

I smiled because every time I outwitted someone of authority, my young pussy jump as if it had a heart of is own. Academically I knew I was out of my depth, but the power of my young pussy gives me the leverage. I deliberately spread my legs wider, letting him see my nut drip out my pink pussy.

I began to unzip his zipper. His little dick moved against the fly, and when I pulled the slider down, it flopped out. I smiled because Dr. Connor had a small ass dick. Even hard his dick didn't reach five inches. His tongue practically hung out his mouth.

"May I?"

Are you serious? What the fuck can you do to this pussy with that little ass dick? I thought to myself.

"Touch, but not fuck."

"I thought you wanted to make a deal?"

"I do, but we got more than enough time to fuck. Doc have you ever rub the inside of some young pussy lips and clit with your big dick without penetrating?" I smiled again when I saw how his little dick sat on top of his hairy balls. The bastard had more balls than dick. I sat on his lap, than forced the head of his dick between my folds, moving it up and down along my crack, carefully.

"Doc, from now on, I want an A on every paper I turn in to you once I register," I whispered in his ear, rubbing my tongue around it. I felt his little dick vibrate against my clit, and then I saw his thick cum squirt around my clit.

"Young lady, as far as I'm concern, you already passed my class." Still wrapped up in his thoughts, Dr. Connors never noticed my cell phone on top of his desk recording his lesson in ethics.

The knock on the classroom door surprised both of us.

I pulled my skirt down and sat back down directly across from Dr. Connors desk with my legs closed. The hand knocking on the door belonged to his brother, Chief of Counterintelligence, Ted Connors, which turned out to be one of the best days of my life. After a few freaky sessions with Ted, he recruited me into the CIA because according to him, I was someone with a different kind of experience, a cold bitch from the hood, in college, with no family.

My first mission for the CIA put Ted Connors in the position he's in today. I was assigned by him to destroy the ring leader of a group of wealthy men who trade child pornography over the internet. Needless to say, Ted Connors took over James Auchincloss business, and I became a trigger happy bitch, one of the best in the field.

Harrisburg, PA...

Charles Krinsky was destine to be the next Governor of Pennsylvania. He was a charismatic Attorney General, who was supported by the current Governor, and all the racist rural county in PA and backed by some very powerful influential people. The only one who can fuck him out the race for Governor was himself, and of cause, me. Yeah, this little dyke bitch here got more secrets than J. Edgar Hoover on Charles Krinsky.

To the people of Pennsylvania he was a white knight, but soon they would find out that all politicians come from the same cookie cutter. I know that there are a lot of powerful people who don't want to see what's about to transpire in the city of Brotherly Love, You see, that's the difference between a soft bitch and a cold bitch. A soft bitch will not go as far as I'm willing to go to bring these perverts down. A cold bitch will beat your brains out at any giving moment. We're going to rock the fuck out, live. And like I said before, Charles Krinsky-he's going down. Like the old Chinese saying 'A journey of a thousand miles, begin with a single step.' You're about to enter the world of the coldest bitch ever.

CHAPTER 1
"Back On My Bullshit"

Presbyterian Hospital...

I sat mesmerized in a private room in Presbyterian Hospital, in the poorest section of Oakland in Pittsburgh, Pennsylvania, feeling rejuvenated, holding on to a secret no one else was privy to.

Two months after AFT agent Ed "Cuba" Sanchez and Sweep Lips were murder, and one hundred and twenty five thousand dollars later, I was ready to finish what the fuck I started.

I walked over to the mirror inside the bathroom and looked at myself. I can't front, a bitch still look good, and hot, even after losing ten pounds due to my surgery, and still, there isn't a fucking discernible trace of human concern or care on my pretty face, because I don't give a fuck.

The stiffness inside the hospital room intensified when I heard the door open and close.

"Ms. Sanchez, Dr. Miller said, addressing me by the alias name I registered into the hospital under. Dr. Miller positioned himself on a chair next to my bed, took a deep, calming breath, and said, "Nice to see you again? From the look of things, you look pretty good," Dr. Miller eyes went straight to my ass.

"I can't complain, I feel good!"

"Good, because now its time for your pretty ass to reward me handsomely."

Could life get any better? It's show time.

"Doc, before I give you anything, I want all my medical records and MRI's, this is non-negotiable."

Dr. Miller stood by the window of the tenth floor hospital room, and gazed out at the people walking into the hospital.

"Listen here bitch! In this hospital, I'm God! I determine who get a successful operation and who don't. "Dr. Miller used the number one trick he'd learned in medical school, lower the patient's expectation, so any marginally operation would be seen by the patient as a work of genius, after all, he only operated on those who could pay for his service.

I sat back on the bed, cleared my throat, and met Dr. Miller's eyes with an expression that spoke terror. Before this asshole could say another word, I began to speak.

"You white muthafucka, you're wrong. In this bitch ass hospital, I'm God! You know why, Doc? Because I determine who live or die," I said as I reached under the pillow and pulled out my home girl, Justice, a heavy 9 mm with a long silencer on it. Without a problem, I aimed for his head.

"Dr. Miller, close your fucking mouth, and listen carefully, I paid you on hundred and twenty-five thousand dollars in cash, so I expect you to at least treat me with some fucking respect, but no, you want to treat me as if I was any spic, bitch."

"But-"

"I said shut your fucking mouth!"

"Doctor Miller felt a sudden chill. He felt as if his bowels might let loose at any moment, and I prayed they would.

Good God, what the fuck is wrong with this bitch? She must be getting her period. I shoulda let her ass die.

"I want you to make sure you understand my dilemma, Doc., before we go any further."

"Absolutely."

"Doc., didn't I asked you to shut the fuck up?"

"Yep!"

"So why are you talking?"

"But-" he said, studying my eyes.

"Shhhh-"

He nodded.

"It means you talk when I ask you to talk. I ask the questions, you answer. Honestly, to the best of your ability. Remember, Doc., I'm God up in this bitch. If I think you're bull shitting me, I will blow your fucking cap back. My bad! Let me say it in plain English so you understand, fuck with me, and I will shoot you in the fucking head. Are we clear?"

"We clear."

"How many people are involved in your illegal business? Who knows I'm here? And where are my medical records? Think before you answer, Doc."

"What the hell are you talking about?" I laughed.

"Okay, let's play your game, Doc."

I was ready to let Doctor Miller feel my pain. I was the kind of bitch who was not about to engage in head games. I've don't stop until I'm satisfied. Sometimes, I have to resort to unconventional methods, but so the fuck what, at least I never have to wonder what would have happened if only I'd dared.

Doctor Miller felt as if he was being choked.

"No one knows you are here. My receptionist made all the arrangement for you to be here, look," Doctor Miller open his leather black briefcase and pulled out a clip board with some papers attached to it, "Here, these are all the documents concerning you. Let's be reasonable. I did you a favor, now you want to bully and threat me by aiming a gun at me," he managed to say.

"Dr. Miller, I'm very disappointed in you. When I get upset, I kill."

"I don't give a shit about you being disappointed. I should've fucked you in that sweet ass of yours when I had you in surgery. However, I did manage to put my dick in your tight, hot pussy, bitch!" Doctor Miller yelled, and then spit in my face.

I know this white devil didn't just confess to raping me, while I was knotted out laying on a table. Naw! Hell naw!

From the corner of his eyes, he saw the door to the room open and he twisted his head around, to see his receptionist walk in. Without another word, and with the spit of that white devil running down the side of my face, I aimed for the receptionist head. Doctor Miller saw the muzzle flash, and actually heard the spit of the shot. The bullet hole was right between the bridge of her long, pointed nose and her hairline. Doctor Miller's bowels let loose on him, and the smell of raw shit took over the room.

"Dammit, Doc, you just shitted on yourself?" He didn't answered.

Oh God, please help me! If you really exist, come in here and save my ass from this crazy bitch, call nine-one-one. Goddam God, do something! In one last effort, Doctor Miller tried to scream.

"Who the fuck is going to hear your bitch ass screaming. Doc? Remember, I'm in a private room. You fagot ass cracker, you are just one more link in the tarnished chain of broken promises. Normally, by now you would've been dead, but since you did me a favor, I'm going to grant you the opportunity to choose how you're gonna die."

"What! Bitch, you're crazy," he muttered as he chewed on his trembling, bottom lip.

"Naw Doc, this is going to be a nightmare. If you don't choose how you want to die, I will take the liberty and do it for you. Now, you could either die like your receptionist, with a bullet hold in your head, or you could try to fly out the fucking window. What is it going to be Doc?"

If I jump out the window, I might survive, but if I let this bitch shoot me, it's over for me. Damn, how can this shit be happening to me? Doctor Miller thought to himself. His body began to tremble violently.

"I rather jump out the window, than give you the satisfaction of shooting me."

"Sure you would."

It's now or never. Dr. Miller tried to grab my arm, only to stumble over his receptionist body, falling flat on his face.

"You stupid spic, I save your life!"

"And I'm about to take yours, asshole! Get up, you weak muthafucka," I said close to his ear, "Or I will shove my gun so far up your ass you will think you're having your first homosexual experience with a long dick nigga. As a matter of fact, stay on your knees, and crawl to Mami!"

"I give you whatever you want. You can have your

money back, I have the money in a safe in my office. Please don't kill-"

"The only thing I want is for you to fly like superman for me. Plus you don't have to give me shit; I take what I want in this life. Now, fly muthafucka! Fly! It's that simple-fly!"

Doctor Miller began to cry like a bitch. Ten stories below, poor Blacks and Mexicans from the near by Urban communities navigated into the hospital in hopes of receiving adequate medical treatment. Many of them would be turned away, because of health insurance. Most of them walked into the hospital with their heads down, unaware of what was about to rain on their asses.

He took a tentative step towards the window.

"Die bastard," I said as I pushed him out. He tried to hold on to the window seal for a fraction of a second, and then he plunged head first, down.

Bam!

The back of his head cracked in half like a fucking watermelon against the concrete. His body convulsed. His eyes were open, as if they were offering him one final glimpse of the heartless bitch who just ended his medical career and life. The crowed below began to pull their cell phones out, snapping pictures, watching the unfolding scene.

I took every piece of potentially incriminating documents with any reference to me, and placed them inside my Coach bag, and then carefully wiped down the whole room. After I was sure I'd removed all trace of me ever having been in the room, I walked out the hospital with a wet pussy. *Damn! I wish Sweet Lips was still here.* I could live with myself, because I think I do more good than harm, plus what other standards any muthafucking body have to judge me by?

CHAPTER 2
"The Coldest Bitch Ever"

The drive back to Philly was short, six hours, but even so I was feeling tense, and trust me, the tension in me was increasing by the minute. Being back in Philly had me feeling horny. *Damn, it been two months since I've had my pussy eaten out the right way. I'm fucking tire of finger fucking myself.*

No one could really imagine what it feels like not having any sibling. I sat in my car for a long while thinking of what I should've done differently. I even tried to remember the happier times I had with Sweet Lips. *The only bitch I really loved had to cross me.*

In my peripheral vision, I saw a dark shadow moving behind my car through the rearview mirror. I grabbed my home girls, Justice, out my bag, ready to squeeze off a few rounds. My homecoming was proving far worse. Despite my enormous appetite for squeezing triggers, I eased down of the front seat of my car, and rolled the window down. When the dark shadow made the fatal mistake of tucking his head inside my car, I pistol whipped the shit out of him and came on myself as I did it.

He shivered.

His front tooth cracked from the crushing blows of Justice.

He shut his eyes, saying a silent prayer. He tried to reach for his weapon, but I was all over his ass like white on rice. He grunted, and rolled, as I delivered a swift, hard kick to his ribs. I jammed Justice inside his mouth, "Don't move, asshole. I've got a real happy trigger finger. Oh shit! Ted, I didn't recognize you."

That's because you're a maniac bitch.

"Why the fuck are you so paranoid? You could've killed me," Ted Connors said, holding on to his ribs.

"You know better than to be creeping up on me."

"Jasmine, you were supposed to report to me last month to begin your new assignment."

"I'm not ready for no new assignment."

"Listen here, you do as you're told, not as you wish. The power that be already consider you a fucking liability, and we both know in our line of work, that's a very unhealthy thing to be considered."

"Tell me Ted, being that you are one of those powers, do you consider me a liability?" Ted rubbed his ribs again.

"No!"

"So then you can stall things for me."

"You are not understanding me. I have no control

over the people you're upset by going AWOL. Plus, that stunt you pulled down here really fucked up a lot of people's money. Now I have people calling me wanting answers.

Muthafucka! You and your associated shouldn't be fucking little kids in the ass.

"I did what I was ordered to do, by you."

"Yeah, but I didn't order you to kill anybody."

"Kill who? I haven't killed anyone yet!" I said with a smile. Right there and then, I knew Ted was not to be trusted. His ass had to be handled, and I knew just how to make Ted forget about what he came to Philadelphia for.

"Bullshit!"

"I'm serious, Ted."

"My sources are telling me that everyone connected with this pedophile case down here, have been wiped out, how ironic is that?"

"Ted, what the fuck that had to do with me? In this line of work people die, so the fuck what!"

Ted shuck his head.

"Jasmine, sometimes you have to let things be the way they are. You have to work with what you have.

I'm sorry, it's over. The agency gave you a year, now it's time for you to go home. Stop trying to be a hero."

"You fucking joking, Ted?"

"Baby, most of the time hero's die, and no, I'm not joking, it's over!"

"You really think it is?"

"They want you real bad, Jasmine, in the fold or in a box."

"Is that a threat?"

"No! A promise." The taste of murder was up in the air, morbid and sticky in the back of my throat. I felt like letting Justice do what she do best, but nah! I wanted this dirty ass nigga to suffer like the dirty perverted dog that he is.

"Damn, Ted, you mean to tell rue you can't stall for me on this one?"

"Jasmine, you're been part of this organization long enough to know how crazy shit can get amongst the power that be."

"Everything I've done been under your orders, now you want to pull the plug on me!"

"The problem is, Jasmine, you have become a loose cannon."

"Yeah but-"

"If I remember, I instructed you to be quiet and fast, about things."

"I have!"

"Now, you have become a liability, a liability bitch!"

If this fagot think he gonna pull the plug on my case, he is wrong. This bitch ass nigga musta bump his fucking head somewhere.

"I understand where you are coming from and

your concern. I just hope you-"

"I'll see what I can do to convince those hungry money thugs to back off your pretty ass. Plus, why are you so adamant about some goddamn, porno?"

"This is bigger than porno! Why don't we get a room at the Hilton, so we can catch up on each other? I don't think we should be having this conversation out here."

"Nah! Hold up baby! In case you haven't heard, porn is legal." His eyes skewed with anger. I knew I touched a nerve.

"Okay, fine, but I can't stay long. I have others associates to visit," Ted said, feeling a cold sweat taking over him.

Once we registered into the Hilton, the wheels in my head started spinning. I had to deal with Ted, now that I had him at my reach, before he puts his CIA thugs on me. There was no doubt that Ted was a cross artist, plus his words kept appearing in the chamber of my head, *they want you real bad, in a fold or in a box.*

"Ted, I need you on this one daddy," I whispered in his ear, while rubbing his dick. I felt heat from the intensity of his stare, which caused my hot pussy to jump in my panties. Although, I rather have me a good, clean pussy to get my freak on, I don't underestimate the power of a long ass dick sliding up in my pussy. You see, I'm one of those chicks who understand the power of pussy, and since I was ten, living in foster care, I understood the power my pussy holds. I don't give a fuck who it is, no man, unless he's a faggot, is going to pass on the opportunity of fucking some fresh, tender pussy. Ted's posture was indicating to me that he was ready to resign to my sexual assault.

"God," he groaned, as I pulled his pants down to his ankles, than pulled his punk panties to the side, letting his nuts hung lose.

"You okay?" I asked with a devilish smile.

"Yeah, I was just thinking."

"Don't think, just enjoy yourself," I said taking his nuts into my mouth one at a time. First the one that hung down the lowest. Then the higher one. Ted was making all kinds of sounds of pleasures. This is the reason why I really don't fuck with niggas. Some muthafuckas make more pleasure sound than a bitch. To me that shit is corny. I like a nigga that makes me respect his dick game. So far, more than often, I find myself fucking niggas in the ass with all kind of crazy, sexual toys, when it should be the other way around. Suddenly Ted pushed my head away, "Put your asshole in my face, I want some action too."

Here we go with the freaky shit, damn! I took my jeans off and squatted over his face. I pushed my fat ass up and down his face. His tongue just tickled me for a moment. I nearly shook myself off his face. This shit was part of the game to get Ted where I needed him to be. I forced my bladder to give up on me, and hot drips of piss mix with blood flooded his mouth. He swallows his bloody Mary as if it was red wine. A twinkling spot of white light shined in his eyes. He appeared to be in his zone, that's why he never noticed when I reached inside my Coach bag.

Spasms of excitement wrenched at my stomach. Sweet, sweet pain. This kill, undoubtably, would be my best. It would send a message to the rest of these pervert, that I have more killing skills than most operatives. I don't underestimate anyone. But since Ted came at me with the bullshit, I'ma assume he is the best they got to come at me, and since I think he ain't, I got to make a believer out of him. I gotta make these assholes know that I am the coldest bitch ever.

Ted was still in the zone, when I reached into my Coach bag and drew out a set of plastic cuffs. With my right hand, I tied his hand to the bedpost.

"Damn baby, you really want to get freaky with daddy, huh? C'mon, give daddy some of that young pussy!"

Yeah! I'm gonna give your sick ass some young pussy muthafucka, *and something else to remember.* I said to myself smiling, because if Ted knew what awaited him, he would've been trying to save his ass.

"You know how I like it, I been a bad girl, I need to be punish, and only you know how I like to be punish, daddy," I whispered to Ted as I reached into my bag again, and bought out a roll of duct tape. I took the fold between my teeth, and tore off a strip, taping his legs to the bottom of the baseboard, wide open. My heart beat a frantic little rhythm and Biggie Smalls song came to mind, *"I got the black talents loaded in the clip, so I could rip through your ligaments, putting fuckers in bad predicament."* Now that I had the subject secure, I got off Ted and put my jeans back on.

"What the fuck are you doing?" Ted blared out when he saw Justice with the silencer staring him in the face.

"Do you know who this is Ted?" I asked him rubbing Justice across his lips.

"Bitch you are crazy! What the fuck is-"

"What do you think this is? I'm giving you what you like, you freaky muthafucka," I responded, slapping another strip of duct tape over his mouth, than I inserted Justice up his ass. The cold metal made Ted asshole wink. Behind the tape that covered his mouth, Ted was mumbling "I'm a bad boy! Oh God I love this." I decided to remove the tape from his mouth. *This punk bitch still didn't 'realized that he was about to die, to him this was part of his freaky games, but oh well.*

"Ted, are you enjoying yourself? Because right now, I'm about done with your ass. It's time for you to die," I said, shoving Justice further up his ass.

"You got to be kidding me, right?"

"Ain't this what you like?" I asked him, while I lapped at his dick head, twirling and whirling my tongue until he was hard as a rock. I needed him hard-I grabbed a scalpel knife out from my Coach bag and place the sharp tip down the crack of his hairy ass, and with one quick motion, sliced his ass in half. Than I grabbed his nuts sack and sliced then open. The warm blood dripped down his ass crack. The nigga yelled as if was getting fucked by a horse. Tears leaked from his eyes. His face squashed against the pillow. I wished he would fight back, kick, or something, but no, he just lay there like the punk bitch he was. I slapped the tape back over his mouth-he felt a warm pink mist, tasted it at the back of his throat. I bought the scalpel knife to his neck, and quickly let it slice across his carotid artery. A horrible, pathetic sound that annoyed me came out his mouth. I touched his pulse in his neck to see if he was dead, than I took the scalpel knife and wrote damage in capital letters across his face. Finally, I let justice do what she do. I pulled the trigger, pumping eight hollow tips deep in the depth of his asshole. I can't front, a sensation I had never felt before came over me. Maybe it was because I was being innovative in dealing with these assholes, sick muthafuckas. I left the room without looking back. I had better things to do.

CHAPTER 3

"Suicide By Cop"

"This is it?" Detective Neal Torres asked.

"Yup," a female lieutenant responded as she observed the body which laid tide to the hotel bed. In her mind, she kept trying to wonder who would do some shit like that. She was trying to solve a fucking crime which had the potential to open a Pandora box of hidden secrets.

Half of her career had been spent down the Badlands, in North Philly, where murder was a normal thing. Not a day went by when she wasn't called out to investigate a homicide. In Philadelphia, most homicides are usually a product of poverty; drugs deals gone wrong, domestic disputes, young niggas playing with guns not giving a fuck about the next muthafuckas, or some jealous ass nigga who caught his wife getting pipe down by some other nigga. If the call would've come from the 39th or 25th district, drugs and gang violence would of been the first assumption, but this case was difference. *Whoever the fuck the victim is, he is not a hood nigga,* Detective Sandra Ortiz thought to herself casting a suspicious glance at Detective Torres.

"People would start coming out of their room soon. You know hotel rooms are on the clock," Detective Torres said with a smile. In the back of his mind he wished he was one of the occupants in the hotel getting his dick wet. His smile quickly faded when he observed a brown skin Latina coming out the room next to the crime scene. He looked around to make sure he wasn't being watched. His heart began beating fast, anger took over his body, he knew his life would never be the same for him again.

"Mari?" Neal Torres said, putting his hand on her shoulders.

The woman turned around not believing the voice she was hearing. After a night of straight up sucking and hard core fucking, her mind was still in the fuck zone. Normally she was an up beat happy whore, ready for whatever, but at that moment, when she turned around and saw Neal Torres, her expression was one of absolute shock. Her lips were moving slightly, but no sound was coming out of her mouth. A few moments of silence passed, then Mari reached into her Coach bag and pulled out her panties, putting them back on.

This is one disrespectful whore. How the fuck I could've

fallen for such a piece of trash! Neal Torres was fuming, not knowing how long he could keep his emotions under control, at least until he gets off duty.

"What the fuck are you doing here, Mari?" He asked, as he blew his nose on a dirty handkerchief he had use on many occasions, to pick up evidence in other crime scenes.

"What it look like, Neal? Don't act like you don't know what I'm into. You met me at a whorehouse, I like to fuck and suck, what the fuck-"

"I guess it's true what they say, huh?"

"You can't turn a whore into a house wife!" Mari finished his sentence with a smile, then added "Nigga you piss on your own balls when you piss! What make you think you can keep this pussy on lock?"

Neal Torres took a deep breath, letting it go slowly. He felt light headed as he realized that what she was spitting out her mouth was true, but it hurt like hell, to hear her say it in such a cruel way. He had never felt secure about his manhood. Even when he joined the police force, he never felt comfortable changing in front of his colleagues in the locker room. He always took a sneak peek at some of his colleagues when they're in the rest room, and wonder why God had to bless him with such a small dick. In his heart, he knew he suffered from little dick syndrome. He used his badge to get pussy from whores in strip Club's, or prostitutes who were willing to do whatever it took to avoid a night in the County Jail.

"Mari, we can discuss this later, right now I have a crime to solve.

Yeah, that's what I thought muthafucka. You little dick ass ain't got no choice but to settle for leftovers. It takes, more than a tongue to make me come.

"There's nothing to discuss! It is" what it is. I love to get smack in the face with a long, hard dick. I love to watch a nigga come all over my face. I love to take it up the ass until it bleed, and we both know you ain't cut for this fat ass. So you either settle for what you already have, which is me breaking your sorry ass off with some pussy once in a while, and you sporting me in your arms when you attend your little police events, or you can keep solving crimes until you find a few criminals."

"Fuck you! Puta sucia! (Dirty whore)."

"Fuck me! The truth of the matter is, that you're the one who should be charged with a crime for having that little ass dick." Neal Torres stared at Mari with pure hatred. He scratched his chin, trying to remain calm.

"You are one dysfunctional whore."

I know, I'm the same whore who got you sprung out on this good ass pussy, nigga." Mari responded, popping two fingers inside of her pussy, making sure they were wet, pulling them out slowly and putting them inside of Detective Neal Torres mouth, then added, "Get a good taste of this pussy, because it's the last time you will ever taste it again." He acted like he was going to throw up, but deep down in his heart; he was willing to play carbon. After all, Mari was the best he ever had.

Inside the room Mari had spent the night in, two males stood in their boxer's shorts ear hustling on the conversation taking place outside their room, unaware that they were in the middle of a crime scene.

In North Philly, Detective Louie Camacho and Detective Adam Cruz were known as male whores, with streets credibility to back up their reputation. It was normal for them to engage in threesome with co-workers and whores from the surrounding strip club's. To them, Mari De La Santo was noting but smuts who loved to fuck men in uniforms, cops in particular.

"Bitch, I should crush your fucking face up."

"What? You gonna play cop and arrest me? 'Cause if you put your hands on me, you're the one who's going to be fuck up. Internal affairs would love to hear about all the punk shit you be doing."

"Nah bitch, I got something better for your ass. I'm not going to arrest you."

Mari cocked her head to the side and continued to get louder with each sentence. By now the rest of the squad members were standing around enjoying the novela that was unfolding.

Lieutenant Sandra Ortiz couldn't believe her eyes. Just days ago, Detective Torres introduced the females in the hotel as his fiancé. *What the fuck is this nasty looking trick doing here? I knew she was a stocker! How the fuck is she gonna be following this clown to work.* Sandra Ortiz smiled to herself. This was one of the many reasons she didn't fuck around with co-workers or anyone with links to the department, well, at least in the Philadelphia police department.

"You see Neal, you calling me a whore, dysfunctional, or whatever else you want to call me don't bother me at all. In fact, it reinforces the belief I've always had about your trick ass."

"What belief, whore?

Lieutenant Ortiz leaned her head back against the wall, closing her eyes. She was enjoying this shit.

"That you are the type of nigga who wear your emotions on your sleeves! You ain't cut for a bitch like me."

Everyone who was witnessing Detective Neal Torres go through this pussy whipped drama, shook their head in total disbelief. When the door to the room open and Detective Louis Camacho and Detective Adam Cruz appeared in their boxers shorts, the whole squad looked, enjoyed themselves. Lieutenant Ortiz, open her eyes and felt her nipples harden. Shit was about to hit the fan, and she was embracing the unfolding drama, as if it was a good episode of the Wire. The temperature in the hotel hallway seemed to rise.

"Cruz! Camacho!" Neal yelled out.

"What the fuck is going on here?" Cruz and Camacho both said at once. Neal Torres just give them both a dirty look, rolling his eyes.

I know this punk nigga is not staring at my dick, Camacho thought to himself, as he tucked his dick back into his boxer shorts.

Why is this chump ass nigga being so dramatic about a piece of whore ass? Detective Adam Cruz said under his breath, still not realizing he was in the middle of a crime scene.

"You two assholes been fucking my lady?" Torres asked.

Are you serious! This whore been through the ranks in the Philadelphia Police Department.

"Yo Torres, stop acting like you don't know what your lady is into. The whole department has ran up in her, without a warrant. Plus, trust me; you don't want to hit that any more, not after I laid this pipe up in her. They don't call me King Kong for nothing, twelve and a half inches, so cut the drama. She's everybody's lady," Detective Camacho looked at Lieutenant Ortiz who appeared to be staring at his dick, and smiled.

"I know how you feel, buddy! If I were you, I would feel the same way. When I was tearing her fat ass up I kinda felt in love with the way she was able to take in the ass. To bad you ain't got enough dick to get up on her ass. She got enough pussy for all of us!" Adam Cruz said smiling ear to ear.

These two niggas must think I'm soft.

"Okay fellows, we are in the middle of a homicide investigation. Torres, if I'm corrects you are still on duty! Camacho and Cruz, both of you are off duty, so I really can't say much, other than, as for this moment, both of you, including the department whore are consider prime suspects," Lieutenant Ortiz said, pointing her fingers at Mari.

"What?" Camacho and Cruz both said.

"In case y'all didn't know, while y'all were sexing Torres fiancé, a brutal homicide was occurring next door. Let me guess, neither of you heard anything, right?"

Everybody in the room knew once the media gets wind of what was unfolding; they would run with it for days. Some of the local media whores would tried to somehow make these decorated homicide detectives seem corrupt, which is how Citizen's of the city of Brotherly love have already dubbed all law enforcement, corrupt to the core.

"You have to be kidding us, lieutenant?" Cruz asked with a serious face.

"You know the drill, amigo! Everyone in this hotel is a suspect. I want both of you in my office in an hour, unless y'all want to give your statement Torres, now," Ortiz was trying to add salt to Torres freshly wounds.

Neal Torres squinted his eyes, *thinking I should just*

teach these assholes some fucking respect. How the fuck is the lieutenant going to ask me to take a statement from these two pieces of shit, she got jokes. Neal gave Lieutenant Ortiz the kind of look which made her palms sweat. With a final grunt, he pulled out his 357 from his waistline and squeezed the trigger. For the next thirty seconds everything went blank.

"Goddamit, Torres!" Lieutenant Ortiz cursed, pulling out her gun, pointing it at Neal Torres head, "What the hell were you thinking?"

"I wasn't thinking," he answered.

Although he had every right to be pissed the fuck off, but as of now, he was just another criminal in the eyes of lieutenant Ortiz, and if he thought she wouldn't put one between his eyes, he had better think twice.

"No fucking joke! Now, put your weapon down, now! Don't make me do this."

Torres rolled his eyes, playing the episode in his head. He looked at the two body's that laid on the floor in front of him and for some reason, he did not seem angry anymore, even though his life as a cop was over. He was silent, obviously still thinking.

"Torres! Put the fucking gun down, now! I'm not going to tell you again."

"And if I don't?"

"Then, you would be joining Camacho in hell! You would not walk out of here alive. I'm not bullshitting you."

"Anything else lieutenant?"

Asshole! I don't give a fuck about your ataque de cuerno (your jealous attack). Now, put the gun down. This is your last warning."

"Bitch-"

POW! POW! POW POW! POW! Neal Torres body collapsed on top of Camacho's body, "You dumb son-of-a-bitch, I told you to put the gun down," Ortiz said, suddenly realizing she was talking to herself. Detective Torres was dead before he felt on top of Camacho and there was nothing more to it.

Detective Camacho die instantly from a shot to the head. Detective Adam Cruz only suffer a gun shot to his dick, which blew off half of it. Mari was left untouched. She sat on the floor with crocodile tears tracking down her face. She licked her lips nervously, as if she wanted to say something.

Damn! How do I explain this one to Chief Rams? Now the Feds gonna want to take over. Shit! There's goes my fucking triumphant moment in the spot light. Lieutenant Sandra Ortiz thought to herself as she pulled her cell phone out and dialed Chief Ram's number.

45 Minutes Later…

Charles Krinsky couldn't believe what he was hearing, the Chief of police in Philadelphia was telling him.

"Charles, I will do my best to keep things under wrap, away from the media until you get here, but we both know how the media is going to get once they get wind of this. They will go south on us.

"I'll be there in twenty minutes with my guys. Keep everyone away, including your guys. Can you do that sir?" Charles Krinsky asked.

"Yes sir, I can do that."

"Good!" Charles Krinsky responded feeling a lump in his throat too big to swallow.

Chief Rams hated having to report to Charles Krinsky. In his book Krinsky was an arrogant, flamboyance asshole who thought his shit smelled like roses, and was only concern with having his mug slashed on the front page of the local News papers. *Fuck Em!* He decided to make a call to his CIA connection which will change the course of things.

It was barely 10:45 am when he reached the Hilton Hotel down Essington Avenue, right behind Philadelphia International Airport. He parked next to a satellite dish news van which was surrounded by a line of police cars.

"Goddamit! I knew it!" Charles yelled to no one in particular. A Fox 29 News helicopter screamed over the

Hilton with the hope of giving the citizen's of Philadelphia a glimpse of what was to become the most sensational murder case the city have ever seen since, the Mumia case. A cluster of detectives leaned against a wall waiting for their next order.

Charles Krinsky could see the chalk outline of two bodies. *Damn, I thought there was only one homicide. Why is there two body's on the floor?* He ducked under the yellow perimeter tape. A black detective held his hand up, ordering him to stop. Charles held up his I.D. "What the fuck are you showing me? This is a homicide scene, no one is allowed beyond that yellow tape," the black detective said not giving a fuck who the white cracker in the suite was.

Who the fuck this black idiot think he is, telling me to stop?

Charles Krinsky didn't hide his anger, "Detective, do you know who am I?" he asked, his tone indicating his displeasure. As Attorney General of Pennsylvania he was one tenacious asshole who didn't like anyone who dare to question his position or authority.

Lieutenant Sandra Ortiz observed the way Charles was turning colors in the face. It was no secret that within the law enforcement community in Philadelphia, white cop's of any ranks didn't like taking orders from blacks in the ranks.

"Sir, I don't care who you think or claim to be, plus I don't give a-"

"Let him through," Ortiz ordered the black detective giving him a stern look, then she leaned forward whispering in his ear "That asshole is the Attorney General, our next governor." The black detective snorted a laugh, "Fuck him!"

Lieutenant Ortiz smiled, than turned her attention towards-Charles Krinsky who was staring at her with an obviously irritated look.

'I don't mean to bring you out here this early, but I was instructed by Chief Rams to brief you on the situation at hand, we have problems," Ortiz said.

"Where is the Chief?"

"He had another emergency call, and he asked me to brief you, since I was the first Senior officer on the scene."

"What's the problem? What! A jealous detective on duty goes crazy and shoot two off duty detectives. Does this require my presence? I hope not, because I have a campaign to run."

"Sir, if you shut your mouth for a second, I'll tell you the problem."

"Who do you think you are talking to?"

"Sir, I really don't give a fuck, nor do I have the time for your prima donna shit. Shut the fuck up!"

"I'm Attorney General, I could-"

"Yeah, blah! Blah! Blah! The problem is you talk too fucking much! Now that I have your attention, I'll tell you the problem you have," Detective Ortiz said, pointing her fingers at his face, than added, "The real problem is, we have a high ranking CIA official tide to a bed with his asshole, nut sack, and neck tore open, and your phone number is programmed on his phone, that's a problem!"

"What?" Charles Krinsky turned towards Ortiz. He did not have a good feeling about this. His life, his career, his hopes of being governor, his marriage, his reputation was on the line simply because some of his most interment secrets were bury within the walls of the same room Detective Ortiz was pointing at. A few weeks earlier he had spent two nights engaging in some taboo sex.

"You seemed surprised, sir?" Ortiz asked, trying to read his expression.

"We don't see much of this kind of homicides around here. I'm sure the media would have a blast with this one," he said, his tone casual. His eyes showed concern, as he wiped perspiration from his forehead with his right hand. He was quiet for a few minutes. After a while he asked, "Run what happened here down to me." Ortiz took her time answering, "He was tide to the bed with duck tape, sodomize with blunt object. His asshole, nut sack and neck was sliced open."

"What else?"

"No defensive wounds or marks."

You dumb spic; didn't you just say he was tide to the bed? That's why he don't have no defensive wounds.

"What else?"

"The strangest thing is; whoever did this poured bleach inside his mouth and on his dick, too."

"Why?"

"Maybe to clean any evidence; bleach means whoever did this has a thoroughly knowledge about forensics. The best way to dispose of physical evidence is with bleach."

Charles Krinsky was so lost in his own thoughts, that he didn't noticed three suited CIA agents standing in front of him. Not wanting to interrupt his thoughts, the lead agent waited until he came out of his thoughts. He seemed surprised when he saw the face of the only women who made his skin crawl.

"I guess you already know we have judicial authority over our man, so I'm ordering you to excuse yourself, along with all these untrained, corrupt, local detectives, from my crime scene, now!"

Charles Krinsky felt silly, with his faggot ass mouth hanging open, but there wasn't much he could do about it.

"Oh really?"

"You know the law, sir!"

Who the fuck is this pretty bitch coming in here calling shots? Dios mio! My God, she got a fat ass. I wouldn't mind licking her clit. Lieutenant Sandra Ortiz didn't consider herself an all out dyke; nevertheless, she did enjoy licking a few clits on the down low, and there was no doubt that the CIA agent in front of her was a triple threat, beautiful, smart and dangerous.

"Let me tell you something," Charles Krinsky said, directing his attention towards the female CIA agent, "I don't know who called you here, but I trust that the local Homicide detectives can handle this case with the delicacy it require," his face flushed.

"Who the fuck you think you are kidding? The last time you handle a case all the suspects ended up dead. You need to worry about your homicide detectives going on a ram page killing each other, about a whore who should be crown commissioner from the way she's been through the ranks. But let me guess, since she's related to your wife she gets a free pass, right? You know Charles, I done my homework. I know things that no one else knows! Spare me the drama. Your locals can handle that there!" The CIA agent said pointing to Detective Louie Camacho who was still laying on the floor with a white sheet covering his body, "And by the way, none of the locals better contaminate my crime scene, are we clear?"

"Yes, we are clear." Charles Krinsky face dropped.

One of the CIA agents open a brief case and bought out an Arc Lamp, which function with a luma-light, that uses metal vapor. This new toy is a hundred times better than a laser. It allows the CIA agents to spot every fucking eyelash, hair, spit, sweat or cum stain anywhere.

"Sir, I'm confidant we will solve this case soon. The CIA forensic people got a bunch of new toys to play with. This Arc lamp is the only one in the country," the female agent said, looking at Charles Krinsky dead in the eyes.

I wonder if they already know I'd been in that room. Why is she telling me about the CIA new toys? Who contacted her so fast? Someone within the Philadelphia Police department must be leaking information. Goddamit! Let me calm down. I'm the Attorney General and I'm getting treated, as a nobody by a spic bitch. Wait until I become governor. Charles Thought to himself.

"No kidding."

"The CIA work fast, that's what you pay taxes for."

"Fuck you!"

"Sir, fuck me is something you would never do. I'm willing to bet, that I got more balls and dick than you, and as you could see, I'm all women."

"I will report you to the U.S. Attorney General."

"In case you don't know, I got more juice than the Attorney General, but here, you can use my phone. I could speed dial his home number for you." The female CIA agent said, placing her cell phone in front of his face, "Don't bitch up now, cracker!" She added with a smile.

Charles Krinsky mouth tightened and he reached into his pockets, but before he was able to pull his hands back out, he had three infer-red dot's aiming at his head.

"Hold! Hold! Hold up, I'm just reaching for my keys I-"

"I wish you would act crazy, so I could show you what this Latin bitch can do with this baby." The sexy CIA agent said, pointing her gun directly at his heart.

Charles Krinsky rubbed his right hand across his nose, "*One day this stinking little Latin bitch will be crawling at my feet. Just wait until I become the top dog in the state.*"

Lieutenant Sandra Ortiz nodded, not sure about what he meant. The only thing she was sure about was getting to know the sexy, CIA agent, who had her pussy hold on fire, dripping, and her nipples harder than marbles.

CHAPTER 4
"Half Bitch Nigga"

Rahway State Prison, Seventh Wing...

Diego Laboca sat impatiently in his tiny cell waiting on his weekly visit. He checked himself out in the small plastic mirror. On visiting days he did the same ritual. He looked towards the bubble where the two, lazy ass guards sat stuffing their faces with jail house made che-che, combined of pre-cooked rice, cup of soup, Ramen noodles soup, summer sausage, and cheese, some buck-eye-jail-house chef, nigga, made for them.

Look at that shit! These niggas ain't got no shame. How the fuck is a nigga going to spent, the money their family sends them feeding these asshole muthafuckas? Dis bitch better get here fast, I'm not trying to spend my day watching this shit.

Diego was stressed the fuck out. Everything for him was going down hill. His appeals in court were denied, his outside connect turned their back on him, once they found out his appeals were denied, and his last hope, his woman Estella, was running around North Philly spending his money, fucking and sucking everything that moved. Diego had seem plenty niggas on lock down get their heart crushed by some whore, but he never imagined that one day he would be one of them niggas, walking around the jail as if he was lost, stressing all day, waiting on the mailman to call his name, blowing up a bitch phone. From day one, the nigga never wanted to face reality, thinking his bitch was going to ride with him. Every nigga in prison goes through what he's going through, the only difference was, Diego is a soft ass, tender dick, bitch nigga. Shit wasn't always this bad for him. At the beginning of his bid, Diego was living lovely, even behind bars. He was considered by the rest of the convicts as being a jail house king-pin.

My cut is tight, white-tee is laid out on the bed. I got my cologne sample from a GQ magazine. I'ma go ahead and rock out with Calvin Klein's Eternity. I don't understand why these crackers don't allow us to have cologne, oil, or after shave.

The phone in the bubble rings! *Come on, let that be me.*

Diego couldn't understand why Estella was acting funny and shit.

Estella was a ride or die chick. At the beginning she made sure Diego had everything he needed. Weekly visits and drug package were unlimited. She even swallowed her pride on visiting days when the females prison guards hated on her, making her wait two or three hours before she was allowed to see Diego.

She had no problem stuffing her pussy with balloons of heroin, or fucking in the visiting room, while other niggas got their freak on watching Diego fuck her behind a vending machine. All that shit change when Diego introduced her to a Captain in the prison who was supposed to be on his pay roll.

Captain Brown was a big black ugly muthafucka who was corrupt to the core. If there was a dollar to be made in Rahway State Prison, he wanted it. Nothing was off limits to him, cell phones, drugs, pimping out female correctional whores to inmates, turning his head away when a nigga was getting murdered. Once his palms were greased he didn't give a fuck who got murdered, or fucked. Money talks and bull shit walks. He was the head nigga in charge, and he ran his prison as if he was out on the block.

"Listen baby, Captain Brown is cool people. Just give him the package and five hundred, that way you don't have to run the risk of getting busted when you come up here tomorrow. You know than hood ratz C.O.'s be hating on you." Diego was trying to convince Estella, but her mind was already made up. As far as she was concerned, this would be the last package he would receive, after today she was gone with the wind.

"Diego, this nigga may be setting you up."

"Nah! I-"

This is an inmate call and is subject to monitoring and recording.

"Like I was saying, Mami, it's safe', so expect a call from him today and-"

"Nigga you gave some cop ass nigga my number without asking me first? You are out of pocket! I hope this shit don't come back and bite you in the ass-"

You have sixty seconds left on your call.

"I see you tomorrow, handle your business Mami!" The phone line went dead. *Damn! I wish I had more phone time left. I love that little whore.*

As the hours passed, and the daily count in the prison was conducted, all hope of seeing his chick on a visit diminish.

Why the fuck this bitch didn't show up? Something musta happen! Diego said to himself as he laid his ass on his bed looking at Estella pictures.

By nine o'clock, Estella was finishing off her second bottle of gray goose. She was feeling tipsy. At twenty four she was hardly prepared to do a bid with her man. She was trying to get her head around, the dumb shit she had to deal with dealing with Diego. *The nigga should've never gotten booked! I got to do me.* She was debating whether or not she should go visit Diego tomorrow or not. Suddenly she heard the door bell ring. *Who the fuck got the nerves to be coming to my crib at this time of night?*

"Who the fuck is it?" She asked, opening the door.

His head was bald, his Obama's large ears were covered with diamonds studs and his enormous fingers were festooned with platen diamonds rings. Although he was an ugly muthafucka, his neatly, trimmed beard added a little bit of sex appeal to his swagger. He was well-built and wore an Armani suit with designer shades. This nigga could pass for Rick-Ross the rapper, twin brother. He looked more like a company executive, than a correctional facility captain.

"I'm Captain Brown and I-"

"I was waiting on your call. Diego never told me he gave you my address. You just can't show up at my crib announced. What if I had company?" Estella knew she was going to fuck him. She knew the second she open the door.

Technically that nigga Diego never gave me the address, I took that shit from his cell. I do what the fuck I want to do.

"I can come back another day if you like me to, but you still got to give me my bread. I care less if you have company or not, I'm here for business." He stepped back, his gaze sweeping slowly up and down her body. *This Spanish bitch ass is out of control! She look like she's got a boxing glove for a pussy.*

Estella tried to rationalize the situation by reminding herself she had eight grams of heroin wrapped up in balloons ready to be deliver to Diego.

"How do I know you're not a fucking undercover pig?" She asked, feeling her pussy hole dripping.

"Are you serious?" His eyes were cold, without emotions.

She looked him dead in the eyes, "I'm serious as a muthafucka! I don't give a fuck if you feel offended or not."

"It I was a pig, you would've been in cuffs already. I'm still standing here, because I gave your nut ass man my word that I would pick up his package. My words and my balls is all I have to stand on." Captain Brown unzipped his pants and pulled down his boxers shorts, grabbing his balls in his hand, "My word and my balls?"

Estella couldn't move. She could barely breathe, and her heart was knocking so frantically in her chest she was afraid, she might pass out. Finally, she'd laid a hand on his dick and was surprise she couldn't get her hand around it. *I don't know if I can handle this one.*

Captain Brown dick stretched out like a flag pole, 13 inches long and fat as a cucumber. From what Diego had shared with him, he knew that Estella was a freak, but he also knew she never been with a black man before, and he was about to change all that shit. After weeks of jerking off with the naked pictures he had confiscated from Diego cell, he was about to get his first shot of Puerto Rican pussy.

Estella licked her luscious lips; her lip gloss had her lips shining to no end. She wasn't sure if she could handle the monster in front of her, but she wasn't no punk bitch, plus, she had a mean ass head game. As soon as she locked the door behind him, she came out of her Rocawear jeans, ripping her pink thongs off herself. She dropped to her knees, bent her head forward and began to lick Captain Brown crown, savoring the sweet flavor of her first black dick. She felt as if she has conquered Africa.

Captain Brown grabbed her head with his large hands and began to fuck her mouth, forcing Estella to swallow six to eight inches at a time. With each push of the head, her mouth stretched. She had deep-throated Diego plenty of times before, but than again, Diego was only packing seven and a half inch dick. As she open her eyes and looked down, it seemed like she had a mile to go before she reached the finish line.

Captain Brown was at the breaking point of busting his nuts down Estella hot throat. Each time she felt his balls jump against her chin; she would push her lips against the ragged hole, clawing back. When she thought he had enough cum up in his sack, she slide her index finger inside his ass, and began finger fucking him, milking his sorotura, making him bust two nut's at once.

"Swallow my black babies, Mami!" He moaned, as he pumped his seeds down her throat in thick globs.

Estella made sure she drained every drop of cum from his dick. Afterward, she withdraw her mouth from his semi-hard dick and looked at him con una sonrisa de puta, with a whore smile, and said "Is that all you got for a bitch?" Then she reached between his legs, cracked his ass cheeks open and, began to eat his asshole doggy style.

Captain Brown felt like a cold blooded bitch, while he was on his hands and knees getting his ass eaten. *How the fuck I let this freak whore put me in a doggy style position?* Although he was feeling all kinds of tingles, he knew he had to take control before he start liking this shit.

"What the fuck are you doing? You like playing with a niggas ass, Huh?" He pushed Estella down on the floor on her stomach, spited a big globule that landed on the tip of his hard dick, spread her ass cheeks wide apart and without warning inserted his dick ball deep into her ass. "Freak ass bitch, talk dat shit now! How you like your ass being play with?" Estella couldn't stand the pain. Her hips flew back, and she began slamming her ass against his dick. Captain Brown knew he had met his match when Estella met him stroke for stroke.

Something snapped inside of Captain Brown. His strokes came faster and harder. His dick was driving Estella crazy with lust. She wanted the same treatment in her pussy. One last thrust, Captain Brown dick swelled, grew to a maximum length, and began to unload his nut inside her ass. Estella was shivering from head to toes and her fat ass began to jiggle like jello.

Captain Brown was buried ball deep inside of Estella ass watching his nut drip out of her. When he pulled out, Estella asshole was stretched open to the size of a golf ball. She quickly got back on her knees and began to lick clean his shitty dick. The whore in her wouldn't allow her to remain lady, like. It was official, she was addicted to black dick.

Damn! I didn't know Spanish chicks get down like that.

"Negro chulo, fine ass nigga, I love this African dick!" Estella said in between licks. Once the dick was clean, she got on top of him, rubbed his dick along her gash until it was on her hot hole. She could feel the large head parting her lips apart. He grabbed her by the waist and lifted her, withdrawing his dick nearly to the head was out, then he dropped her hard on his dick. Each drop was met with a squishing sound which only made his dick harder. Each time he touched her belly button from the inside, Estella would feel a different thrill. Captain Brown was definitely touching untouched territory.

"Mmmmmmmmnnnnnnnnn!" Estella moaned in pleasure, feeling as if she was being split in half. Feeling Captain Brown stretch an extra inch, Estella pussy contracted around his dick. The dick was so good she began to squirt, (cumming). Captain Brown was feeling super extra knowing he just made the wife of one of his inmates squirt all over his black dick.

"Damn nigga, I guess I'm a nigga loving-bitch now!"

"Señorita, mi mami chula, once you go black you won't go back," Captain Brown said, slapping Estella on the lips with his dick.

"Yo know negro chulo, I love to fuck, so are you going to keep this chocha, pussy popping? Or is this a one time thing?"

"I know you ain't catching feeling about some dick."

"Nah! I just like to know where I stand on the dick side of things."

"I'm here Mami for as long as you want me-"

"You better, negro chulo."

"So what about Diego?" Captain Brown asked.

"Fuck Em! That hermaphrodite, half bitch nigga can't compete with your dick, plus, he got a ten year bid."

"Hold! Hold! Hold! Hold fuck up! What did you just say? Hermaphrodite!"

"Yeah, hermaphrodite! I thought the prison knew. Diego was born half bitch, that's the reason he be acting funny, the nigga is half bitch, for real."

"I always thought he was a funny cat. Fuck him! He is a fool for getting knock off, leaving your Puerto Rican freak ass out here alone, his lost is my gain," Captain Brown said formulating his next plan.

Outside of Rahway State prison he was just another

typical nigga on the grind, but inside the walls of Rahway he was Jesus Christ, Allah, Muhammad, whatever God a nigga thought existed, in Rahway, he was him. When he throw his Captains white shirt on and walked the corridor in the prison, he felt like God, plus, the ass kissing niggas who flocked around him made him feel important. Every slick ass nigga who thought they were using him to get their package inside the jail got their prayers answer. Their wifey, whore, hoodrat, baby mom's, cousin, sister, girlfriend, or mother always ended up leaving their love one behind and riding the Captain Brown dick express.

For two day's straight after being introduced to some black dick, Estella sat in her bathtub soaking her stretch pussy in vinegar trying to make her pussy tight again.

CHAPTER 5

"Blood on My knife or Shit On My Dick"

A Week Later...

Diego kept trying to dial Estella phone number, and every time he got the same message, "The party you are trying to call don't wish to receive collect calls".

"He waited until they called for yard and went on the hunt for Captain Brown, *maybe he'll let me use the phone in his office. I know this whore didn't put a block on the phone.*

Captain Brown was observing Diego from his office on the security monitor. In fact, for the last week he'd been avoiding Diego on purpose. He wanted Diego to know that in Rahway State prison, he was nothing but a punk ass bitch. He was breaking him down mentally, and it was working. Within a week's time, Diego went from a pretty boy, to looking like a fucking street bum. Unshaved, hair uncut, missing meals, not showering, and jonesing for the love of his life.

In prison nothing goes unnoticed, and niggas on the Seventh Wing started to notice how Diego was acting. Walking around spaced the fuck out, talking to himself, acting as If he was new to this shit. One old head in particular paid extra attention to Diego. *Look at his ass walking around here like a lost puppy,* Tito Matraka thought to himself as he jerked off in his cell door, watching Diego.

Tito Matraka was a lifer with over thirty years in the system, and a vicious appetite for some young ass. He was an expert in pin-pointing out soft ass, tender niggas. At 6'4", 280 pound of solid muscles, Tito knew not too many muthafuckas in Rahway wanted to stand in his path.

"What's popping young buck?" He asked Diego, pulling out a pack of Newport's, offering him one.

"Nuthin' much. I'm goin' through a little sumptin', nuthin' major."

"Do you want to talk about it? From time to time we all go through, something! I'm here, if you want to talk about it," Tito Matraka said with a concern face.

"I'm just dealin' with some issues, Ol' head."

"Listen here! You know I never been a fag! I'ma keep it one hundred with you. Young buck, you smell like pure shit, and you look like a fucking street bum. I'm sure whatever you are dealing with ain't that serious. I'm not gonna have any young buck walking around here smelling like shit, that would be a bad reflection on me. If you need soap, shampoo or whatever, I got you. Come up to my cell-".

"Yeah! Yeah! I just gotta take care of some bizz with Captain Brown, I'll be up there to talk to you, alright!" Tito Matraka eyebrow rose slowly. He couldn't wait to discover if Diego was a hermaphrodite for real. Captain Brown had given' him the green light to do as he wished with Diego.

"Umm, hum, whatever, just don't forget to come to my cell. I really want to talk to you," Tito said, shaking his head emphatically.

In front of the Seventh Wing, Captain Brown stood watching the inmate line movement returning from the yard. Many of the inmates mean mugged him, others just walked by calling him asshole under their breath. None of that shit meant anything to him. He was God in Rahway. When Diego saw him his eyes shined with hope. *Thank God dis nigga came to work, Diego mumble to himself.*

"Capt, I been waitin' on you, what's poppin'? Do you have may shit?"

"It's customary to make an appointment to talk to me," he said as he stared Diego down, daring him to say some dumb shit.

"I see you have an attitude, today, huh?"

"Nah, I don't have an attitude. What is it that you want?"

"I want my package, the shit I paid you to go pick up at my crib."

"What package?"

"Yo sun, stop playing!"

"Playing! The game has changed. From now on, drugs are not allowed in my institution. I'm running a drug free jail.

"What? What? You're burning me for my shit?"

"Captain Brown wouldn't do that. I'm just letting you know about the new rules, plus, Estella never gave me the package, but you wouldn't know that either, because she put a block on the phone."

"How da fuck you know?"

"Trust me, I know. I know, because I had my dick so far up in her Puerto Rican ass, when she called the phone company and put the block on. Understand this, you hermaphrodite freak, Estella is no longer your woman!" Captain Brown was spinning a set of hand cuffs around his fingers, looking at Diego as if he was welcoming the chance to use them.

"It's all kosher, Capt. Everyone take a loss once in a while. I guess today is my turn," with no hope that Captain Brown was going to give him his package, Diego walked away. Under the circumstances he was in, there wasn't shit he could do.

"Exactly! I could make it very inconvenient for you in here, Diego," Captain Brown yelled.

Diego footsteps echoed on the dirty prison floor, even the sound of other screaming inmates seemed muted. He needed to be in a private sanctuary, but he also knew his celly was probably watching the Maury Show or Jerry Springer, so he decided to pay his old head Tito Matraka a visit. *Maybe Tito can talk to Captain Brown about my package. How the fuck Estella gonna do me dirty like dat?* Diego thought to himself as he stood in front of Tito Matraka cell with a God-help-me-look.

"Jesus! What the fuck is up with you?" Tito asked him, as he thought to himself. *It's gonna be a long, ugly day.*

"I'm just stress da fuck out. Captain Brown did a nigga dirty! I paid him five hundred to pick up a package for me at my chick's crib, and the nigga burned me, on top of dat, he blew my chick's back out."

"Did you talk to him?"

"Yeah!"

"What he had to say for himself?"

"He told me to get da fuck outta his grill! Dat my chick belong to him, and dat I was burned."

"Yeah, well, it ain't always fair in this place. That fool been burning muthafuckas forever up in this place. What the fuck can you do? Nothing! You either, strap the fuck up with a shank and take it to his ass, or you bite the bullet and take the lost, either way the ball is your court," Tito said with a strange smile.

"Man, I'm tryin' to go home!"

"So stop bitching! You see little nigga, there are rules to this shit! You either man up and fight for yours, or bitch

up and get punk'd out," Tito said, his voice shaking with
hostility.

"Can you help a nigga out?" *I thought you'd never ask.*

"Can I help? What I look like to you, a dog? Plus my
help ain't free. What's in it for me?" Tito asked, closing
his cell door, putting the using the toilet sign up, than he
threw a red towel up on the door to block anyone from
looking into his cell, than he added, "Young buck, I gave
you the benefit of the doubt, but I see you're a cold bitch,
so I'm going to treat you like one," Tito said, punching
Diego dead in the face breaking his nose and knocking out
a few teeth. Diego fell to his knees. Tito hit him again, "Get
up," he yelled or "I'll break your jaw."

Diego met the promise of violence in his eyes, and
thought better to stay on his knees.

The truth of the matter was, Diego had always been a
bitch ass nigga. The last fist fight he had was when he was
ten, and even then, he got his ass crushed. On the street,
he fronted like he was that boy, because he had a team of
hard niggas who would move out for him, but in Rahway
State Prison, he had to fend for himself, and today, he was
being tested by one of the hardest nigga in the jail.

"I thought we were cool, ol' head?" Diego eyes
widened as he wiped his mouth with a shaking hand.

"Young buck, you're a soft ass nigga. So I'm gonna
break it down how this shit is going to work. From now
on, you are my people, my bitch, and since you won't fight

for your shit, I will."

"But I'm not into-"

"It's gonna be a long, ugly day. You could either put blood on my knife or shit on my dick." Tito Matraka said, placing a thin Plexiglas shank under Diego's chin.

"Damn, ol' head, we both Boricua!"

"Man, I ain't trying to hear that Boricua shit! Blood on my knife or shit on my dick?"

If I can't beat them I might as well join them. I'm not trying to die inside dis place. Fuck it, so be it. Who da fuck gonna know anyway? Life isn't easy, and it sure as hell wasn't fair.

"I'll be your bitch ol' head, but you got to promise me you won't put our bizz out in population. I'm not try in to be a piece of meat for all the lifers," Diego responded, fear sliding down his spine.

"I'd got your back, young buck, I'm serious. Whatever it takes, I'll make sure Captain Brown gives you back your package." Tito felt a surge of pride. Booty-bandit had been bred into his genes.

Diego dropped to his knees. He embraced Tito Matraka and burst into tears.

Jesus! This nigga really into this shit! Tears! Damn!

"Diego pressed his hot, little lips against Tito Matraka dick and sucked, like no one he'd ever knew. After twenty minutes his mouth tasted like shit.

Somewhere in the back of his mind, Diego knew there had to be someone, who could loaned him a shoulder to cry on, or give him a word of comfort. He couldn't believe or accept the fact that he just sold himself out, to the devil out of fear. I know I can't be such a bitch? How da fuck I ma just let a nigga run up in me raw? He felt dirty just thinking about it.

I leaned back in my chair mumbling to myself the words to Diddy and Dirty Money's new song "Hello! Good morning! Hello," before I could finish singing the sound of my phone interrupted my thoughts. I answered the phone with an attitude.

"What!"

"This is a collect call, from a state correctional institution, at Rahway State prison, to accept this call please press 4, to hear the charge of this call please press 2. All calls are subject to recording and monitoring."

Who the fuck got the balls to be calling me collect from prison? I thought as I quickly pressed 4 to accept the call. I learned a long time ago that a lot of usable information can be collected from prison; muthafuckas in there run their mouth too much. Inmates would tell stories to try and impress other niggas. Others would straight commit a joot, robbery, by stealing another niggas life style and identity. Some would even go as far as purchasing girl flicks, from the back of the XXL Magazine, write their name on the back, and front like some hot chick mailed them to them. I even heard of some muthafuckas confess to crime they never committed just so that they could appear hard core in front of other niggas. If a person is not hip to the game, he would believe half of that shit. One thing for sure though, in every jail, there is that one nigga who specialize in ear hustling, collecting information with the hope of getting a get-out-of-jail free-card.

"Hello?"

"May I speak to Inez?"

"May I ask who calling?"

"Diego Laboca, hello?"

"I know who you are, what do you want?"

"I need to speak to you face to face."

"About what? As an informer you're no good any more. I can't send you money in prison. In fact, don't ever call me again, because-"

"Wait! Wait! Wait! I don't need money I want to get out of this place."

"Nigga, as I stated, I can't help you at all!"

"I got sumthin' nice for you. I got a smut DVD with a few influential people gettin' their freak on. Trust me, dis shit will quench your thirst." There was silence on the line for a long minute.

"How do I know you're not bullshitting me on this? I need to see it first, before I can offer you my assistance."

I wonder who the fuck is on that DVD.

"Write dis address down. 2345 North 6th Street. In the basement, behind the washing machine there is a metal box, look inside and you will find a DVD. I have some more, but you can't get those until I'm out dis place; we got a deal or what?"

"Give me a name?"

"Put it this way, dat cracka runnin' for Governor in PA is on it, I don't know his name."

"Give me some specific names."

"Nah, baby, dis is all I got to deal with."

"Diego, anything you tell me is confidential."

"I wouldn't give a fuck if is not! I just want out of this place, before I gotta put shit on some nigga dick! I want out of here!"

"That sound like a problem. If you' don't give a fuck, then drop a name or two for me. Nigga, if you want out of that place, you better start getting your snitch game up, cause' if you don't you will definitely be putting shit on some niggas dick, now give me a name?"

"Let's just say, I got some shit on DVD that can destroy many people's lives. From Philadelphia, New York, all the way to Puerto Rico. Some muthafuckas may even commit suicide, others straight up would try to have my head, but I don't give a fuck, I need to bounce from here, can you make it happen?"

"I can use my juice card if I want to, but why should I? Right now, I don't have shit but some snitch calling me on the phone, with some alleged information on some influential people. My question is, what part do you play on the tape? Who recorded it? When was it record? And what's on the tape?" I knew this snitch would keep talking, if I made him feel important.

"You know, I been bless to have been born half bitch, and I know how to use my boy pussy well. I do what I do, to make my way in big places, view the tape for yourself," Diego said, feeling the tension ease.

"You know we're not supposed to be discussing deals until the district attorney approve it."

"Use your juice card! Plus, I got some shit on that uncle Tom nigga too! Like I said, view the tape for yourself.

"Really?"

"Really! If you don't like what you see, after you view the tape, I won't bother you again."

"One question Diego, what are you lock up for? And how the fuck you ended up in Jersey?"

"Long story, but the short version is, I came to Jersey to visit my old lady's people, traffic stop, got pop with half of brick and a burner."

"I feel your pain, but if you know how to use your boy pussy well, why are you scared to put shit on a niggas dick?"

"You got jokes huh?"

"I'll be there to see you tomorrow afternoon-"

"By the way, one quick favor, I need you to call da

jail and have them place me in (P.C.), protective custody. Officially, I'm your informant-"

This call is subject to recording and monitoring. You have sixty seconds left on your call.

"Consider it done! Plus-" The phone line went dead.

Captain Brown was sitting in his office not believing his ears. He replayed the recorded conversation back, and still was in shock to know that Diego Laboca was a government informant. That spelled danger for his business inside the prison. *I'ma just wait until his contact visit him tomorrow, for the meantime he's going to be fed to the wolves.*

CHAPTER 6

"Breaking And Entering"

6th Street, North Philly...

Once I got off the phone with Diego LaBoca, I drove down North Philly to the address he had given me. I sat in my car watching the scenery, which was decorated with all kinds of lowlife muthafuckas, a perfect match for my mood.

I was parked across street from the house, close enough to get a clear view. I observed the movement on the block and smiled 'cause there no place like home. The streets of Philly raised me, to be the bitch I am today. If I wasn't a CIA agent, I probably would've been a hood rat, running around with no sense of direction.

As I sat in my car, I notice an expensive Blue Jaguar with New Jersey plates on it. "What really put me on guard was that the big black nigga had on a "New Jersey correctional officer uniform, but the yellow Spanish chick had on a Fiesta Black dress which accentuated her fat ass. *I hope Diego ain't trying to play me.* I thought to myself, as I watched the big black nigga and the Latin chick walked into the house. From the way the girl was grabbing on dude's dick, some fucking was definitely going to take place inside that house. *Damn! Now, I got to sit out in this bitch, and wait and see if these two muthafuckas are going to stay in the house, or bounce after their done fucking. I don't wanna have to go in my bag and body both of them, damn!*

After an hour and a half, they both came out the house and hopped back into the Blue Jaguar. I reached under my seat and found Justice, my 9mm, and shoved her under my shirt into the back of my jeans. I hopped out my car and strode slowly to the house.

I went around the back of the house, moving deliberately through the alley. I glanced into each window, as I past and saw no indication that no one else was inside. I kicked in the back door, opening it with one kick. Once, inside I shut the door behind me. Breaking and entering isn't beyond my reach. As I made my way to the basement, my pussy began to jump in my panties. The house looked like any other house in the Badlands; dirty and reek of piss, not quite what you'd expect from a fly bitch with Fiesta dress or a nigga who was once pushing weight.

The exception was what might be called the fuck room. The smell of pussy wafted through the air. It was large, living room size. In addition to the obviously new flat screen TV, it was also furnished with a new bedroom set full length mirrors, an entertainment center with all kinds of video equipment on the shelves that, took up most of one whole wall. It was obvious that the two characters who, just left were doing some serious fucking.

I spotted the washing machine in the corner, neatly covered with a blanket. I reached behind and immediately discovered the small metal box as Diego said. I opened it, and two DVD's jumped out at me. I picked up the remote control, turned the TV on, flipped the DVD into the player, and to my surprise, Charles Krinsky face popped up on the screen. My gut tightened another notch. This shit was the kind of thing, where the headlines practically wrote themselves. Even though I started sweating, I kept my gloves on. I decided to take the DVD out the player and check the whole house. After searching the basement, I made my way up to the living room. The most interesting thing I found in the living room, was a roller dex with names and phone numbers, of some very influential people. I made my way upstairs to the bedrooms. I found what I was searching for inside a trash can, which was over flowing with discarded empty Chinese food containers. I emptied it out on the floor, and out came four more DVD's. Diego must've thought no one would look in the trash can. I fought with the idea of going back down to the basement, just to see what was on the DVD's.

I have many peculiar qualities, but being stupid was not one of them. I understand how serious shit can get, if the occupants of the house returned back and caught me inside. *Fuck that! I already got what I came for.*

CHAPTER 7
"The Last Respect "

Look at this pathetic shit! The Givnish Funeral Home was packed to the gill, with Ted Connors family and colleagues.

Lines of men and women in uniform, and hundreds of CIA agents, from different part of the county were dressed in neat blue suits. Motorcycles of Philadelphia police led the way. Flags around the City were flown at half mast. These people just don't know that their home town hero was probably the biggest child molester in the country. *Damn! I wish I had my cell phone with me, so I could snap a few pictures of my work. Now, I know how an artist feels when he create a master piece, and the masses embraced it.*

The entire city and surrounding counties were talking about the murder, of Ted Connors. Not much was said about Detective Louie Camacho, being gunned down, by one of Philadelphia finest.

The CIA is law enforcement's crown jewel, and from the look of things, it was losing its luster. *This is just the tip of the iceberg. Wait until I unleash the beast in me.*

I walked into the funeral, still amazed at how people react to death.

Peter Newman and Sidney Weldon, both recognized me the second I entered, and made their way towards me.

"Hey! What a surprise," Sidney said, putting his hand on my elbow. I was surprise at this gesture, but I remain calm.

This muthafucka got balls to be putting his hands on me.

"Why would you be surprise? I'm here like everyone else, paying my last respect to a great man," I responded with a little smirk.

"You don't mean it."

"Sure I do. The question is, what are you doing here?"

"I don't have to respond or answer questions to those beneath me. I'm the authority figure here."

"That being the case, then this conversation is over Amigo"!"

"Bullshit!" Sidney Weldon said, in a harsh whisper voice that probably echoed through the funeral home. He took a step towards me, but I wasn't intimidated.

Sidney Weldon had spent the vast majority of his career, behind a desk in Northern Virginia as a fucking analyst writing reports. He had a PH.D and was smart in a bookish way, but when it came down to doing the dirty work, he was a pure pussy. This bitch ass cracka never done a tour in the war zone.

Despite his training at the farm, he had never distinguished himself to be anything more than a dick rider, a lapdog, who rise in the CIA ranks, because of Ted Connors. *Them two muthafuckas were probably dicking each other down. If he only knew, what I got on his ass he be trying to be a friend to me.*

"Cracka, you ain't got the cojones to put your hands on me! Come on, I like it rough."

"Stop it! Have some respect for Ted, that's the least you could do," Peter Newman said, glancing around. A group of people had gather around trying to get a glimpse of the side show.

Sidney Weldon took a few breaths, trying to calm himself down. He wanted answers. He needed to know, if I knew something about his involvement in Ted's Child pornography business. All the dramatic shit he was doing was nothing but an act. He was such a bad actor; he couldn't muster a single tear.

"You think you can scare me?" I said, in a raspy voice.

"Where were you last Friday?" Sidney asked.

"What's this a Q & A session? But if you care to know, I was in none."

"None where?"

"It's none of your fucking business! You know the

protocol for meeting and questions." I was mentally fucking with this cracker. I knew my alibi was air tight, but fuck him! I needed him to be at ease. I wanted him to feel as if I knew something, which I did, but I wanted him to slip and fall, so I could have a reason to crush his ass.

"I want answers! Fuck this protocol shit. You were the last person who saw Ted alive. He came to Philadelphia to see you," Sidney yelled, unable to remain calm.

They want you real bad, in a fold or in a box. Ted's words kept ringing inside my head. He came to Philly to see me. Sidney just answered my question. Ted was going to kill me! He got what he deserve. In the fold or in a box! Well, we already know who's in the box.

"I Haven't seem Ted in months. I've been away on sick leave. I just got back to the city early Saturday morning. I understand you're angry, but remember, we're on the same side of the law. I feel the same way. Ted was like a father to me. He is not the first and won't be the last person to die in the line of duty."

"You don't want to fuck with me, bitch I will-"

"What? You will what? Reveal my identity? Asshole, in case you don't know, my identity is protected by law."

Sidney Weldon licked his lips, "Fucking, dyke, bushwhacker, spic," he paused, lookin' over at Peter Newman expecting a reaction, obviously irate that there was none. Sidney didn't have no qualms about hiding his prejudices.

"I know a man of your statue, isn't intimidated by my sexuality? After all, you are a close-door homo. Maybe if you was in tune with your sexuality, you probably wouldn't have to hide behind your job. Everyone knows you're a booty-boy."

"Peter! I want her debriefed, now!"

"Sidney! You can't debrief an operative without the proper protocol," Peter responded, playing it safe, trying not to get caught up in the bloody mess that was about to jump off.

"I don't like her swagger and arrogance. She needs to be stripped and retrained with a sense of mission and purpose."

"That sound personal to me! Too bad I don't have to answer to you, sir!" I said with a smile. Throughout the entire conversation with him I kept my gaze steady on him, my body in a slight forward lean. I knew if I turn my head, or looked away, or move my hands, he would conclude that I was lying. He couldn't figure me out. I'm too good at what I do.

"Okay, let's stop this now. We are professionals. Plus, the President and most of his cabinet had just arrived. I believe he's going to deliver the eulogy," Peter Newman shook his head, than added, "We could all ride together to Arlington National Cemetery."

"You and Sidney could ride together, I have things to do. I can't make the ride."

"Peter, fuck that spic bitch, she's not one of ours. She don't know what loyalty is, plus, Ted wouldn't want a piece of shit like her at his resting place."

I smiled, because Ted's resting place wasn't his decision, it was mine. In life Ted Connors always prided himself of being a Negro, from North Philly who made it to the top of the law enforcement elites, the CIA. He loved to be amongst the short callers in Washington. Now in death, he could definitely be proud to be amongst dead presidents, Supreme Court Justices, five star generals, and other famed assholes. In my eyes, Ted was an in-the-way-uncle-Tom-nigga who got caught slipping.

His name would forever be remember upon, the CIA wall of Honor, where a plaque will be hung next to the others CIA agents who had lost their lives.

"Sidney, you are a very passionate individual, but watch yourself, make sure you don't end up being a major addition In Arlington next to Ted," I said with a smile, walking away before he could respond.

CHAPTER 8
"Sweet As Honey"

I got to have that fly bitch! Lieutenant, Sandra Ortiz thought to herself, as she observed the theatrics bullshit Sidney was putting on. When she walked out the funeral home, I knew I had to make my move. I spotted her walking towards her car. Damn! She's driving a Benz? I follow her a few blocks down Market Street, before I decided to go on the great pussy hunt.

"Shit!" I hissed when I saw the flash of blue light behind me. I slowed the car down, pulling over at the corner of City Hall.

The detective took her time getting out of her car. I reached under the front seat of my car and griped Justice and my I.D., letting Justice rest on my lap in plain view, keeping my eyes on the unmark car. *This pretty hoe got heart to be following me like she's crazy. I noticed her watching me inside the funeral home, now she wants to play police and make a traffic stop. I should just push her wig back. Bitch better want something.* I thought to myself as I watched the detective get out of her car, and walked towards mines. When she reached the passenger side of my car I held up my I.D.

"What's the problem officer?" I asked sizing her up.

"There is no problem. I'm Detective Sandra Otiz and I-"

I interrupted her, giving her a questioning look. *This bitch look like Stacey Dash!*

"If there is no problem, then why are you following? In fact, you been following me the minute, I enter the funeral home. Do you know me? Do I know you? Cause right about now I'm feeling some kind of way about you invading my space."

"No I don't know you, but after tonight I will. This is not an official stop, this is a personal stop! You can put that thing away, ain't no need for it, at least not tonight-," Detective Ortiz said pointing at Justice with a horny ass smile, making sure I saw how hard her nipples were. I won't front, I wanted to bite one of them muthafucka right through her blouse, her nipples were staring me straight in the eyes.

"Excuse me?"

"As I said, after tonight you will know me better."

"Detective, this is illegal."

"Then arrest me!" Detective Sandra Ortiz open the first four buttons of her blouse, and popped one of her tits inside my car, being brutal about her approached, than added, "We are both grown! Go ahead take a taste of this good ass nipple. If you don't like what you see, then you can drive away, and for what I see, you are wondering whether or not you should put my nipple in you sweet mouth. As stated, you could drive away or you could arrest me!" Detective Ortiz said, rubbing and pinching her own nipple.

"Arrest you, huh?"

"Either that, or you could follow me back to my place." I blushed like a young virgin girl. After all, it had been a while since I got my freak on.

"Where do you live at'"

"Germantown and Lehigh Avenue, across the street from the Second Hand Store."

"I'm a virgin to this!" I lied. This Stacey Dash look-a-like had my pussy wetter than a muthafucka.

"Good! Then I'll break you in. I won't do nothing you won't let me do."

I stared at her speechless, wondering where this was going to lead. Normally I'm the one who take charge, but today I was willing to play the timid role. I wanting to see if her pussy game was a brutal as her approach.

She wasted no time when we got to her house. I felt a tremor of excited apprehension race the length of my spine.

"Come on Mami, I want you so bad" Detective Ortiz said, between kisses, leading me into her bedroom. Once in the bedroom, she began to take off my cloths. My shirt came off first, than my bullet proof vest, baring my exquisitely shaped, pink nipples, which were ready to be sucked. Obviously growing impatient, Detective Ortiz stripped me of my jeans and panties. She dug her hand into my pussy and cradled my clit.

"This is gonna be mine," she said, she left a trail of kisses on my nipples.

We embraced, our tongues tangling with each other, our eyes half closed, out tits pressing softly into each other body, nipple to nipple. Detective Ortiz raise her right leg and snake partly around my body, her thighs parting so that her partly open, wet pussy could press against my thighs.

"Come on, lie down!" She ordered me. She leaned down and took one of my stiff, big nipples into her mouth and began to suck. The stimulation of her hot mouth turned my nipples a strawberry color.

I threw my head back and closed my eyes. Ortiz reached for a honey jar on top of the night stand. She unscrewed the top, dipped her fingers into the golden brown sweetness, and rubbed it on my nipples. I gulped.

What a freaky bitch! She spread my legs wide open and poured honey down my clean, shaved pussy, and started licking my chocha, pussy clean, not bothering to count calories.

"Don't stop, I love your lips!"

"Don't beg baby." Then she moved her hot mouth down my thighs until she reached the thick outer lip of my pussy. I writhed with delight and frustration. I reached for Justice on the night stand and gently placed it on the back of her head.

"Oh...Come on... Come one bitch! Come on! Don't torture me...Eat this fat chocha, Mami, or I blow your brains out!"

Startled by my word and action, Ortiz parted my pussy lips with her thumbs, completely opening up my inner depths.

"Aaaaaaahhhhhhhhhh..." I moaned, my back arced as my pussy got invaded by Ortiz tongues which, was lashing out to burst itself far up my chocha. When she sucked my tender pink center into her mouth, I went half crazy with lust.

"OmyGod!" Was the only thing, I could muster up to say. She was inching my clit softly.

"Oh please..."

"A pussy like yours deserves the best. Mmmm, such a hot pussy."

My body heaved upward from the bed, it surround

her tongue and sucked it in. I needed it. I couldn't understand how a thick tongue was driving me out of my elements. Ortiz slid three fingers into my wet chocha and her thick thumb in my asshole, damn! that shit felt good.

"You like that, Mami? In your chocha and asshole at the same time? It turns you on, huh? You like getting finger fuck in the front and the back, right?"

Her tongue, finger and thumb performed a miracle. I didn't want this shit to end.

"Hmm, oooh, I love it."

When it come to satisfying an asshole, a hot Latin tongue is better than a dick or finger.

"I'm coming! I'm coming!" I pulled my knees up to my shoulders and jutted my chocha and culo, (ass), forward to Ortiz greedy mouth, and passed out, as she made me come through my asshole.

When I awake the next morning, Detective Ortiz was ghost. I gather my clothes, got dress, tucked Justice into my waistline and took my slippery ass home.

My cell phone started ringing off the easy, the second I walked into my apartment. Eight of the calls were from Diego Laboca. I wasn't in the mood to talk to a dirty ass snitch, so I let his call got to the voice mail. I already had in my possession what Diego thought he could use as a get-out-of-jail-pass, the DVD's.

On my list of undesirables, he ranked number one. From my point of view, Diego was nothing but a snitch bastard, who been on my pay roll for years. Leaving him in prison is the right thing to do, and in the process I be saving a few lives. There's no fairness in this game, it tit for tat.

CHAPTER 9

"Fed To The Wolves"

The P.A. system was buzzing with "Inmate Diego Laboca, report to the bubble." Diego was in Tito Matraka cell trying to keep him out of his ass, but Tito has been given the green light, to deal with Diego which ever way he saw fit.

"I spoke to Captain Brown, and guess what?"

"What?"

"I got your package," Tito said, pulling out three balloons of heroin from his pocket, putting them on top of his Sony TV. "I told you I would look out for you."

"Yo! I appreciate dat ol' head," Diego said with a new sense of hope.

"Inmate Diego Laboca, report to the bubble!" Diego was acting as if he never heard his name being called over the P.A system. Tito smiled to himself 'cause he knew he had Diego right where he wanted him, sitting on his bed, getting ready to get his boy-pussy busted open.

"Nigga! I got the package, so that mean I own this shit, unless you are willing to make me an offer I can't refuse," Tito said as he tore open a Snickers Bar, sizing Diego up.

"You can keep half, ol' head."

"Do you hear yourself! How the fuck you gonna offer me half of something, when you ain't got shit, nada! You musta bump your head somewhere. The only way you gonna get this shit here is, if you give me a shot of that boy-pussy or fight for it. Man fuck that! Either way I'ma get that. Matter of facts, I'm done with the rapping," Tito said, as he graded the three balloons from on top of his TV putting them inside of his foot locker, then he reached under his bed and grabbed a wooden floor brush and started beating Diego over the head with it. The first two blows knocked Diego the fuck out, cold.

He laid Diego on his back, took his brown issue pants off, ripping his punk panties off with excitement, throwing Diego legs over his shoulders, penetrating his Matraka, (dick) as far as it would reach inside of Diego boy-pussy.

"Damn, Carajo! Fuck! This is better than a piece of ass," Tito couldn't control himself. He's been away from real pussy for so long, that the tightness of Diego boy-pussy had him busting his nuts within the first ten strokes. Diego boy-pussy was so good that he by-passed tearing his asshole open.

He took Diego shoe lace off his brown boots, and strangles him with them. Afterward he threw Diego 125 pound body inside of four plastic trash bags. He left his cell and got the recycling trash can, which has wheels on it and brought it up to his cell. After he made sure none of the cell block snitches were around, he threw the plastic bag which contained Diego body, in it, and pushed the recycling trash can down the cell block, as if nothing had happen. When he reached the bubble, he asked Captain Brown to escort him to the back dock, so that he could empty out the recycling can. Once in the back dock, Captain Brown watched with a smile on his face, as Tito threw the bag inside the electronic, trash compressor, dumpster, and with much delight, he pressed the button to crush the trash into a pile. This was one way the Department of Correction ensures no inmates tried to escape by hiding inside of the trash compressor.

Diego became another fatal statistic on the landscape of America prison system. No one would mourn his death, not even his trifling ass woman, Estella.

Washington, DC...

About the same time Diego life was ending in a trash compressor, in Washington, DC, Sidney Weldon was returning to his rented apartment from a night out with his underage lover. Like most people within the CIA community, Sidney was beginning to hear the rumors on why Ted Connors was murder, and with great interest and sinking despair he began to panic. Sidney had thought he had it made, until he was informed by Ted, a week before his death, that a CIA operative may be responsible for leaking information on their extra-curricular activities.

He walked up to his apartment. As he opened the door, his private cell phone on top of the table began to ring.

Ring! Ring! Ring! Ring!

What the fuck! He thought. A few people in the agency had his private line number. The only purpose anyone would use it, is if something had happened that would require his presence.

Man I'm hungry! He ignore the phone ringing and walked into the kitchen and open the fridge, taking out a container of left over Roast-pork, throwing it in the microwave oven, and after two minutes the smell of the pork filled his nostrils. Two things he loved the most, was the smell of his young lover and pork.

Ring! Ring! Ring! Ring!

Who the fuck could be calling me? He looked at the phone and saw that the caller I.D. was unavailable, and thought about not answering, but he decided to answer it, only to stop whoever was calling him from blowing up his shit all night.

"Hello? Who is it?"

"Shame on you Sidney, not recognizing my voice." I said with a smile. I knew Sidney was trying hard to put a face to the voice.

"Do I know you?" He asked his voice cracking.

"Of course you know me! Damn! Four days ago you was talking all crazy from the side of your neck to me at Ted's funeral."

"What do you want?" He asked in professional voice.

"I just wanted to remind you that Arlington National Cemetery have enough space for you."

"Bitch! Do you know who I am? I will have you fired from the agency! Arrested! Locked away for life. I know you killed Ted."

"You sick pervert! You ain't gonna do shit to me. Yes! I killed Ted! Fuck him, and fuck, your wife, kids, grandkids, and whoever else looks to you. I don't give a fuck about you."

"You spic bitch-" I didn't give him a chance to finish. He was already on borrow time, so I just hung the phone up.

I would have her arrested, tonight; Sidney Weldon pushed the speed dial button to his private phone line to call Peter Newman.

They found what remained of Sidney Weldon on the sidewalk of his apartment building next to a pile of dog shit, because the blast that exploded inside his apartment delivered him there. The instant he pushed the speed dial button a tiny spark from his phone ignited the gas that filled his apartment, gas his sick ass wasn't able to detect, because he still had the smell of his lover sweaty balls in his nostrils. It took two hours to extinguish the fire, which destroyed the whole building, and claimed the lives of eight innocent's neighbors. His demise inflated my ego. To kill a man so respected, in all, law enforcement cycles, had my pussy on fire.

CHAPTER 10
"The End Justifies The Means"

The greatest virtue of humanity is mercy. This is what these white muthafuckas would feed the general public when it comes down to excusing one of their own, when they get caught with their pants down, but in this book, everyone get the same treatment.

I'm far from being a moralist. I'm a dyke, I love me some pussy. Yes, I'm guilty of that sin. Some may think I'm too outrageous with my shit, but would you say the same, if it was your daughter, son, nephew, or grandchild getting rape and explored by these sick ass, politicians? Destroying our young children future is one of the greatest sin anyone could be capable of committing. So, why the fuck should I cordial? I hate them bastards! I hate my foster parents! I hate Dr. Miller for raping me, while I was on the operating table. I hate them for how they destroyed the fabric of civilization.

Having been a victim myself, I know the faces of these merciless assholes. I know who they are. These sick muthafuckas had built their fortunes, while breaking the laws they had sworn to uphold.

I live by my own set of rules. I'm on a crusade to stop child exploitation, lethal judgment always get the job done, a complete banishment from this fucking world, evil deeds to crumble into forgotten dust, is the only satisfaction that can put me at peace, other than that, I let Justice do what she do. How else could a cold bitch like me deal with these perverts?

Fuck em' all, ain't no one exempt from my brand of justice.

A Week After The Funeral...

At ten thirty sharp Peter Newman stepped into Charles Krinsky world.

"Charles, good to see you. Would you like some Tea? I don't, do the coffee thing any more."

"I'm not here to socialize; I'm here to talk business."

"You know Peter, when I was a Democrat, you and I were good friends, now it seems like we on the opposite side."

"You're right! These days, we are on two different roads."

"First of all, Peter, I done nothing to you, personally."

"Yes you did, you sold out to the Republicans!"

"It was a political move."

"Okay, what's the problem?"

"The problem is that, I feel like I'm being ostracized by you and the rest of the guys."

"Actually, I was thinking the very same thing. I cannot bring myself to accept the fact, that you been so careless in your extra-curricular activities. You are the reason Ted Connors and Sidney Weldon are dead."

"Dead?"

"What part of dead did you not understand? Sidney apartment was blown into pieces this morning, and your finger prints are all over his car. In fact, a fucking rubber full of your cum was found in his car, your DNA is all over the place. Now, how is you going to explain that, to me?"

"Look Peter, this is getting pretty far afield, isn't? It an insult to hear you make, such an accusation towards my character."

"You should be praying that I don't arrest your disloyal ass, for murder. I have enough evidence on you to buried you under the fuckin' jail, so don't play stupid with me. I hate your political ways, but I like the man in you, therefore, I'm granting you the opportunity to explain yourself."

"Peter, we all know Ted and Sidney were both closet homosexuals. Sidney was a reactionary bigot. Whatever they did on their spare time in none of my business, Sidney and I went back to D.C. after Ted's funeral and yes, we did a little socializing with a few girls. I had sex with one of them in Sidney's car. I might of taken off the rubber and left it behind, that explain why my finger prints were in his car," Charles Krinsky said, trying to remember everything he did when he was down in D.C. *Damn! I just left Sidney alive! Someone is trying to set me up, who? Why?*

"Where were you when Ted got murdered?"

"I really don't remember. I believe I was with a friend, maybe, I don't know, I don't remember."

"Charles, you are running for governor of Pennsylvania, so if I was you, I would start remembering things, because if you don't, it can cost you in the long run."

"What are you trying to tell me, Peter?"

"Charles, we both know evil doesn't wear horns or a tail to signal that it's with us." Charles Krinsky frown deepened.

"I'm confuse, Peter."

Peter Newman knew he had an advantage on Charles; watching the play of emotion across his pale face, had Peter on cloud nine.

"Put it this way, Charles. I have every reason to believe that, whoever murdered Ted and Sidney, may come after you next. It's gotten personal."

"Personal."

"Yes, personal!"

"But-"

"Listen, I'm very aware of all the late nights parties, and all the sex tapes you have made, engaging in some very incriminating position with under age kids," Peter said, a tinge of bitterness creeping into his voice.

"Those are pure speculation and guesswork. I never have done such a thing."

"I don't have time to play this game with you. I just want you to ensure me with a sense of certainty, that you are clear. That nothing throughout your campaign is going to pop up, and change the course of things?" *I've been studying you close, and I'm very much aware of your every move. Sooner than later, you will have to face your mistakes, and what comes with it. I know your M.O. already.*

"Peter, I been under the radar, I'm clean."

"Charles, I'm not going to pussyfoot around. I need to know, have you ever been sexually involve with Ted?" Peter asked without a flinch in the eyes.

Charles felt sick to his stomach, he felt like Peter was stepping way over the line. He wasn't sure if he should answer or not. *Should I be truthful with him, or should I just chalk it up and let him come to his own conclusion? Who the fuck was he to be asking me about my sexual encounters.* Charles thought to himself as he looked at Peter, eyebrows lifting.

"No!" Charles respond. He was feeling the weight of the world on his shoulders, but he trusted Peter somewhat, because after all, Peter has inherited Ted Connors list of contacts.

"Listen, from now on, stay clean. We have a lot of money invested in your campaign. We need you to win."

Peter Newman was beyond himself as he made his way back to Philadelphia from Harrisburg Pennsylvania. The special recording device he had implanted under his right arm was so small no one would've seemed it even if they would've strip him. The device was not known to the public, and the manufacture was strictly controlled by the CIA. The real reason he decided to wear the wire was to record Charles Krinsky dumb ass. He wanted solid evidence, audio always sounded better, when accompany with some good visuals.

That Same Night...

"After November 2, 2010, election', I will be promoted to fill in Sidney Weldon vacant position. I was informed by the United state Attorney General, yesterday," Peter Newman said, as he sat in front of my computer in my apartment.

"That's a wonderful thing, Peter, the agency needs

more people like yourself in position, plus, you already paid your dues, I'm happy for you-"

"Us!"

"Us?"

"Yes, us, I decided to recommend you for my current position."

"Peter, thank you, but no! I love to be in the background. I'm not cut for the office. I like to explore the country. I'm happy with just being who I am, today."

"Sooner or later, you will have to move on to new assessments!"

"Wait a minute, Peter, what are you saying? If I'm correct, we had a deal, right? I do your dirty work and in return, I do my little clean up amongst these perverts in the agency. So far, you are the only one who benefited from all this."

"True, but you never mention to me, that you're little clean up mission would put the lives of some of the agency most prestigious members on the line. I mean, Ted is dead, Sidney been blown away, my brother-in law, Judge McCall is dead, not to mention the rest of the low life's who never made the obituary. When does it all ends?"

I knew that, as soon as this asshole got his promotion, he was going to put shit in the game. I got something in store for his ass.

"It ends when I'm done cleaning our backyard up! I'm not done yet! There are still a few perverts; enemies who need to be disposed, right now, I don't have a clear conscience,"

Peter's face became graver; he hesitated for a second and said, "You better clear your conscience up soon because, after November, I'm running a clean agency, are we clear?"

Cracka! You better hope you get to see November.

"You're the boss now. Peter," I said with a smile. I bit my tongue, because talking to this asshole was a waste of my time. By his own distorted belief, Peter viewed himself as being untouchable, but I was to prove him wrong. This cracka must've forgotten that I'm the enforcer of the law.

"Now that we clear, we need to focus on our next target," Peter said incredulously. He had no idea how far I would go to defeat my enemies. I'm not the type of bitch who will submit to the will of another person or a government agency.

Peter played the tape he recorded of Charles Krinsky incriminating himself.

"He basically confessed to having a sexual relationship with Ted, this shit is good. The media is going to have a blast with this one," I said soothingly.

"How you coming along with the DNA sample you collected?"

I have a perfect match, to none other than Charles Krinsky. I have enough to build a solid case against him, today."

"Let's give him enough rope to hung himself. Right now he feels safe. He believes I'm going to protect him. I want to make the RICO stick, all the way back to when he was a District Attorney. This is the kind of case the RICO laws were created for. At the end of all of this, you will receive a medal from the President of the United States.

"Peter, don't take this the wrong way, but medals and recognition means nothing to me."

"Don't worry baby, the end always justifies the means."

That night, I sat in front of my computer putting the finishing touches to the photographs that, would soon become an Americana, collective item.

CHAPTER 11

"It Was All A Dream"

The dream was like poetry in motion. It had me ready to scream.

The vision.

The smell of Sweet Lips turned my stomach. I felt her eyes staring at me. Her touch was real, throat clogging reality. I felt as if I was paralyzed. My new kidneys felt like they were on fire.

"Inez?" Sweet Lip's appeared at my bed side, seemingly out of the smoke. "Why? Why? Just tell me why?"

"I-I can't. I mean, I don't think I can-"

"Inez, you're all I had. I'm all you're had. Do you understand me?"

I felt awoke. I was conscious. Damn! I'm tripping! But I couldn't move. Sweet Lip's voice kept sounding off in the chamber of my mind. I wanted to get up from bed and go about my daily business, but Sweet Lip's smell was overpowering my whole existence, plus, my kidney 'was beginning to hurt. Badly.

"You shoulda never robbed me. I trusted you. I loved you, and you had to go on and cross me as if I was a fucking nut, bitch, fuck you. You're dead! You don't scare me."

"Stop trying to justified yourself. I tried to tell you that I was your biological mother, and you still killed me, why?"

"But-"

"But what?"

"I'm sorry!" I said, as if apologizing was going to allow me to get the much needed sleep my body was demanding. Sweet Lip's vanished as quickly as she had come. The conversation had lasted only a brief minute, but even so, Sweet Lip's presence had my heart intensifying. I had to be dreaming! I sat up in bed unable to breath for a moment. I felt as if I had ran a mile. *Lord forgive me, but if the bitch was really my mother, she shoulda told me from the get-go.* A cold wind sweep through my bedroom. I felt asleep.

I tossed and turned from side to side. I felt someone choking the air out of me. I was fighting, but the grip got tighter. In front of me was an open coffin trying to suck me in it. I reached under my pillow and pulled Justice out, squeezing off a few rounds. I curled up in my bed staring around at the room. The feeling on my shoulders felt as if the world was pressing down on me. I had to be dreaming.

"Shit! What the fuck you mean you can't find her?"

"What part of I can't find her don't you understand? I'm doing my best to help your broke ass. I'm using all the resources at the station, but it seem as if this trick disappeared from the face of the earth."

"First of all, you better watch the tone of your voice when you talk to me!" William said, making a fist and putting it right through the mirror, cracking it pieces.

"Nigga, you called me for help, I ain't call you. Maybe you need to leave them hood ratz along than you wouldn't have this problem."

"Bitch! Just do what the fuck I ask you to do. Find my bitch! I need to know if she was really pregnant."

"Then you shoulda kept a leash on the whore! Fuck you and you're slick ass mouth. As matter of fact, if you want to find your bitch, you look for her your damn self"

"Wait!"

"Fuck you!" *The dick was good while it lasted, but I don't have the time to be getting caught up in some baby drama shit.* Sandra Ortiz thought to herself as she replayed in her head how she was going to lock down some fresh pussy. *Niggas out here now days got too much drama for me.*

Puerto Rican Day Parade...

The Puerto Rican Day parade in Philadelphia was in full swing. All the Puerto Rican chicks were out in packs looking for a trick to bag. Me personally, I don't never miss a parade for shit. A lot of potential good pussy would be on exhibit.

I stood in front of a group of girls who were having a reggaeton dance off, down 5th street, which is where the parade ended at, but it's also where all the Ricans in North Philly stay at. We don't march with the parade downtown because too much shit be popping off. Police be fucking with people, looking for illegal immigrants to arrest. Although it's our parade, then gringos, whites folks, be acting like its their parade, so we stay down North where we could burn them threes, and basically do what the fuck we want without having to worry about the police. The gringos stay away from North Philly on the parade day. The shown bunnies who do come down there, come down there with the understanding that they gonna suck and fuck and than bounce back to their white community.

Once the parade past the Parkway you know it's on and popping. Puerto Rican flags hanging in front of house. Salsa music blaring from every Spanish Bodega. Bellacas, hood bitches, showing what their momma give them. Pretty boy niggas showing casing their dicks. Old head bitches out in pack trying to compete with the young girls.

It's was just a beautiful day to be Puerto Rican and alive.

As I'm standing on the corner of 5th and Indiana Avenue enjoying the day, an old man brushed by me, his shoulder grazed my right tit, but since there was hundreds of people standing around I let it slide. But then the old man started staring at me as if he had a problem with me.

"Viejo, old men, why don't you move yo' old ass so, I could watch the parade. Yo' blocking my view."

"Jasmine, it's me," he replied, keeping his voice gentle and easy, tapping himself on the chest.

I felt like spitting on his face. I looked at him again with pure hate in my eyes, but instead played off.

"Papi!" I asked surprised.

"Damn girl, you don't recognize your own father?" *Muthafucka, are you outta your mind? Father!*

"What the fuck happen to you? Last time I saw you your nasty ass was like two hundred and fifty pounds. What's up with-"

"Your mother is doing fine, como siempre, like always, fat as hell, but overall, we are still caring for the needy. Damn! can Papi get a hug?" He said as he putted his arms around me, basically taking a hug and a free feel against my will, because he let his left hand slide slowly down to my ass.

The nerve of some muthafucka! Once a pervert always a pervert. I thought to myself. It must be a great day to live because, if it wasn't for the people enjoying the parade, I would've blown his top off. It's been almost four years since; I last saw my foster parents, and just staring at this pervert brought back bad memories. My pussy hole started to lick, and my trigger finger was shaking. *Calm down bitch. This old pervert will get what he deserves, one day.* The little grimy bitch in my head was speaking to me. Suddenly, a young girl who couldn't be no more than fifteen years of age walked up to him, grabbing his arm, giving him the poppy-eye look.

"Please...Papi, can I get a few dollars so I can buy a flag," the young girl said.

I wondered where she came from. Who she was? Was she a young prostitute trying to sell some pussy? Whoever this young chicken was, she was engaging in a dangerous game with no rules at all.

The minute I looked at her, I instantly knew that my foster father was laying some serious pipe in her.

"Yanira, meet your sister! Your older sister." Don Rodriguez said with a smile. I felt sorry for heir. Yanira mouth curled up at one corner and she winked at me. Suddenly my curiosity felt prurient. Why did I want to know more about her? Why did I wanted to know how she ended up in my foster parents care?

"How long have you been living with them?" I asked Yanira, staring at Don Rodriguez with a disgusted look.

"A year and a half," came the sweet voice of a child.

"Do you like it there?"

"It's better than being in the system."

"Why?" I asked already knowing the answer. Yanira just shrugged. "At least I got a place I can call home, with a mother and father."

I knew this old pervert got this young girl believing that he's the best thing that ever happen to her. I thought the same way when I was under his care. I know his fucking her! I was feeling dizzy. If I rescued this chick, she would be loyal to me. I looked at Yanira in her eyes and I could see the cry for help sign glittering. She looked helpless. I felt like I was losing my marbles, feeling sorry for a chicken off the street that I just met, but I knew fist hand the monster that was lurking over her was vicious.

"Listen, Papi! Why don't you let Yanira hang out with me for a while, so we can get to know each other, better? I will make sure she gets home sound and safe," I said, leaning forward and whispering in Don Rodriguez ear, "If I find out that you are fucking this girl like you done me, I swear I will hunt you down and kill you! You better pray I'm wrong!" His eyes widened. He blinked twice. Shockingly he understood everything I said, specifically the last part. I knew that the next time I laid eyes on my foster father, he was gonna wish it was a dream. I was determine to put a stop to his little dirty deeds towards young girls.

CHAPTER 12
"Like Mother Like Daughter"

"What'd you have in mind, hon?"

"Nothing much. We're just gonna hangout. Get to know each other a lil'. I'm mainly interested in knowing what's really good with you."

"What do you mean?" Yanira replied, acting all stupid and shit, but I read right through her young ass.

"Listen here, Yanira, let's cut through all the bullshit shenanigans." Her eyes widen, and her coffee colored eyebrows shot up. I took a good look at her. Yanira was stacked. The little bitch had a banging ass baby like Nicki Minaj.

"Huh?"

"Are you gonna talk to me or what? Cause if you gonna at all funny with me, you could fucking bounce."

"It's along story," Yanira replied with watery eyes.

"I ain't got nowhere to go, what's up?"

Mari De LaSantos was an unfit mother by every sense of the word, and by any standards put forward for a mother. If an award was ever to be created for unfit mother's, she would be the winner. She was a striper slash prostitute with a client list that would put Wikkileak out of business. There was no shame in her game. She sold pussy by the pound. Her only love in the world was money, and there was nothing she wouldn't do to keep herself relevant in the stripper cycle. She was every hustlers dream and every daughter's nightmare. At thirty-six years old Mari De LaSanto's didn't play by the same rules that every other stripper must obey. Win, lose or draw, this whore didn't give a fuck about no one. She was content with being who she as, the top whore for hire in the Philadelphia Policy Department. The only obstacle in her path was her fifteen year old daughter.

This lil' bitch is in my way, she gota go! If she thinks I'ma take care of her all the time, she got something else coming. I'm out there fucking and sucking, stripping and letting all kinds of niggas run up in me, and dis lil' bitch wonna sit around the house as if she was a diva. I'm about to expose her to my reality- her fate. Mari thought to herself as she was bent over a desk in the 39th District in North Philadelphia, while Detective

Adam Cruz was tearing her fat ass out the firm. After the detective empty his balls up in her, he sat on his chair with a limp dick, smiling. "Damn! Your asshole feels like it got a mouth of its own," he said, smoking a Newport cigarette.

"If you think my ass is good, wait 'til you get that big dick of yours in my daughters ass."

"Stop! Stop! Stop! Seriously, Mari, do you hear yourself? Bitch, I'm a cop! Do you know what they would do to a cop in jail for rape?"

"Rape!"

"Yeah rape! Your daughter is only fifteen years old! She may look twenty one, but in he eyes of the law she is still a child. I'm not even going to play myself out like that," Detective Cruz said as he got up from his chair and grabbed some tissues out of a box on the window seal, ready to wipe his dick down.

"But she's fucking like a wild rabbit. Plus, I see the way you be looking at her ass when you come over to my place. Don't act like you ain't trying to hit no young pussy-"

"She could be fucking like wild rabbits, but she won't be fucking me. Like I said, niggas go to jail with football numbers for that kind of shit."

Dis clown wonna act all righteous about some pussy, knowing damn well he'd a freak at heart. I got down on my knees, took the tissues out of his hands and threw them in the waste basket and stared sucking his hairy balls greedily and hungrily with my hyperactive pink tongue. I let his shitty dick rest on top of my nose. When I finally detached my mouth from his balls, I gripped his dick in my hand, kissed the crown and asked him, "Are you gonna do dis favor for me. I want you to treat yourself to so young pussy," I wrapped my lips around the crown of his dick and looked up at him. I knew I had dis nigga in the palm of my hands, ready to commit murder if I asked him to do so. I'm sorry sisters, but a whore got to do what she got to do. I haven't run across too many of you black sisters who would swallow a shitty dick right after it comes out the butt- hole. This is a dirty dog world, and I'm playing for keeps.

"Mmmmmmm-whatever you want baby, just suck my dick," he moaned. I tongue whipped his dick as it was a run-a-way slave. I squeezed his dick again, triggering him to splash my face with his cum.

I don't give a fuck what anyone says, every nigga in this fucking world love to see their own cum splashing on a bitch face. All y'all young bitches better step your game the fuck up. If any of you young bitches want your man to come off that paper or if you want your man to cop them new Dolce and Gobbana boots for you, let him come all over your face and you will see how fast he would come off that paper. I drained his dick so good and let cum trickle down my chin that he was ready to propose to a bitch.

"Mari, you are too much. You might be the hottest

dick sucker in Philly."

"I let my lips do what they do. Now are you going to do me that favor or what?"

"I got you Mami, I be over to your house about nine o'clock."

"You better, because I want my daughter to learn how to respect the power of the dick. Trust me, Papi, you gonna love it."

"That's the problem! I'm trusting you too much. I'm not tryna get whip on some young pussy. You wouldn't want me to trade you off for some young pussy. Would you?"

"It would never happen! You and I both know, not too many bitches out here gonna treat you the way I do. I ride for you nigga, now it's time for you to ride for me."

"If you say so! I'm only doing this because I got love for you. Just keep in mind, I don't do no half stepping shit, so I'm going for the whole package." .

"It wouldn't be you if you didn't. I expect you to do you."

Two Hours Later...

Mari De LaSantos had a big ass smile from ear to ear. Detective Cruz has arrived half hour earlier ready to fuck. He stuck two E-pills up in Mari asshole and she was beginning to feel the effect of it. Her asshole was on fire.

She was beyond herself. She had successfully and sexually had manipulated one of Philly finest into doing her dirty work.

"C'memr, Yanira!" Mari yelled, at her daughter.

"Espera un momento! Wait a moment!" Yanira responded while she looked at herself in the mirror.

"Heifer! Get your ass down here, now!" Yanira ran out her room in some booty shorts and a wife beater, leaving nothing to the imagination. There was no doubt, she was built like her momma-thick in all the right places.

"What's up, mom?"

"Listen, what's dis I'm hearing you been hanging around boys. I'm gonna ask you one time and one time only, are you fucking?"

"No, I'm still a virgin." Yanira responded in a shy tone. Even though she had let a few boys in school lick her young honey box, she had never let anyone, finger fuck her or straight up lay some pipe in there, yet.

Dis lil' bitch must've think I'm stupid or something. I know she been spreading her hips. I'ma find out tonight.

"I'm also hearing you been smoking a lil' weed!" Yanira kept her eyes gaze fixed on the floor, as if she was embarrass to look at her mother-She was terrified.

"Yeah, I only tried it once," she bashfully admitted.

Tell me something I don't know.

"Here, tried dis!"

"What?"

"Since you already be smoking weed, I rather you smoke in here with me than in the street. I know you are gonna keep trying it, so why not do it in front of me."

"But mom!"

"Don't worry baby, you are almost a women." Yanira didn't realized that she was about to receive the ultimate high, one that would change her life forever. Unbeknownst to her, the shit she was about inhaled into her lungs wasn't weed-it was wet, pcp.

"Light dat shit up baby," Mari said, as she handed her daughter a lighter and a Philly blunt, laced up with wet.

"Damn! This shit is good!" Yanira said as she inhaled the smoke from the blunt. After the first six puffs the wet had her seeing shit, hearing voice, and feeling horny.

By the time Detective Adam Cruz walked out the room with his dick stretch out, Mari had her daughter stripped, laid out on the couch. Detective Cruz couldn't believe his luck. He looked at Yanira and smile. He than pinched her nipples and watched them swell up like marbles. He slid his fingers deep into her' young pussy.

"Oooooooo," Yanira let out, her body tossing in tantrums of lust.

Dis lil' bitch is enjoying dis shit. Mari thought as she felt a little bit of jealousy running through her veins.

Yanira respond only made Mari angrier. Once Adam pulled his finger out her pussy and slid them into his mouth, he tasted something salty. When he saw the little spot of blood, he couldn't contain himself.

"Mari, you didn't tell me she was a virgin," he said, surprised. The last time he had virgin pussy he was in high school, almost twenty years ago.

"Dat bitch ain't no virgin, she probably on her period. You punk ass nigga, treat yourself. Put you dick in her, now!" Mari said, hating on her own daughter.

"Oh, trust me, I'm gonna put in her pussy, and ass, but first I want to start with her mouth. In fact I want you to join us. Take your muthafucking clothes off and help me teach your daughter how to suck a big, good ass, long dick."

In no time Mari was on her knees butt-ass naked helping Detective Cruz guide his dick into her child's mouth. Once Yanira lips caressed the thick shaft, Mari started sucking his balls.

Detective Cruz was beyond himself as he watched his entire dick disappear down Yanira throat. It was clear to him and Mari, that Yanira was born for this type of action. *This is a dream cum true. Mother and daughter at the same time! Goddamn! How many niggas can say they experience this kind of shit?. Oh shit, her lips feel incredible, better than her mothers.*

"Mmmmmm, suck my dick, shorty! Deep throat me like your momma do. I wanna come down your virgin throat." Minutes later Yanira had hot cum dribbling from the corner of her mouth. She tried to open her eyes, but could not focus. Her world seemed to be spinning around in cycles. She was seeing three of everything.

Marl made sure he stayed hard, sucking on his balls as is she was sucking on two grapes.

"Get off my balls, bitch; and grab your ankles." She did as she was instructed.

"Mmmmmm," Detective Adams Cruz let out, feeling the wet lips of Mari wet pussy against his dick. He slid into her until hilt. Than with one quick motion he pulled out of Mari, and stood over Yanira for a second, undecided where to start, than he turned Yanira over on her belly, spread her heart shaped, fat ass apart. For a second he thought about popping her virgin butt-hole, cherry first, but he couldn't hold back. He needed to feel some super tight pussy around his dick. Even though he had broken the seal with his fingers, his dick was still met with some resistance as he entered her. The sweet tissues of her young virgin pussy had him at the breaking point. He was trying to hold back in order to adjust to her sweetness, but he couldn't. He felt like a kid in a candy store. Since he couldn't risk getting this young chick knotted off, he slowly pulled out of Yanira and without warming; he began to press the head of his dick into her asshole. He pounded her ass out the farm.

"I'm gonna come in your ass, now!" Mari looked at her sweltering daughter becoming a woman right before her eyes. Yanira fainted. When Yanira awoke an hour later, immediately she felt the soreness between her legs.

"Bitch! Who da fuck was you fucking in my house?" Mari yelled acting as if she was completely oblivious to what had transpired.

"Mom I wasn't doing nutting...I...I..." Yanira didn't know what to say. All she remember was passing out right after her mother had given her a blunt to smoke. Next thing she knows she's waking up with a burning pussy and a busted asshole, licking with a thick, sticky cream that she had no idea what it was.

"I! My ass! Since you want to act like you are a grown ass woman, pack your shit up and get the fuck out my house, now!"

"Mom, where I'm suppose to-"

Bitch! I don't give a fuck where you go. Da only thing I know is that you got to bounce, now!"

"Can I at least pack my things up?"

"Is you deaf? Is you crazy? You ain't got nutting in dis house. Everything you own, I bought with my money! Now, get the fuck outta my house before I whip your ass. As a matta of fact, you are leaving with what you got on nothing." Mari wanted to humiliate her daughter in a way that would make her fend for herself, so she did it the same thing her mother did to her, putting her daughter, asshole naked, out the house.

Yanira stood on the corner of Germantown and

Indiana butt ass naked for hours until a good ass, perverted old man offered his assistance.

Once Yanira told me how her mother did her dirty, and how she had to sell pussy to survive on the streets of North Philly, I couldn't stop the tears from escaping my eyes.

"So I guess my foster father was the Good Samaritan who picked you up from the streets."

"He rescued me, gave me a place to lay my head at night. He even went down to the social service department and got legal custody of me. In return, I break him off with a little bit of pussy here and there, plus, I let him keep all the money he receive every month. I never ask for anything cause I hustle everyday," Yanira said looking me straight in the eyes.

"I feel your pain, and I could understand why you out there giving up the pussy for a few pennies. As of today, you can stay with me."

"You're sure I can stay with you?"

"Yanira, if I didn't want you to stay with me, you would've been out my car already. I'm just asking that you don't lie or steal from me. Also, you don't have to sell your body at one of them dirty, ass titty bars." Yanira tossed me the coldest and the most indignant look she could muster.

The little bitch stared me down as if she wanted war. I tried to
sort through the chaotic confusion of the moment. Here I was
rescuing a chicken from the grip of evil, my foster father, and she
gonna cop an attitude because I told her she didn't have to sell
pussy. This little bitch got issues.

"How am I suppose to eat? I'm too old to be depending
on any one for anything. I like to have my own bread to
spend." Yanira said to me with her arms folded as if I was
speaking in Chinese.

Absolute silence followed.

"Baby girl, I'm about to teach you a new hustle, just
have a little faith in me, okay." I felt my jaw tightening,
and my pussy hole began to leak. I fought against it, but it
was fruitless.

"Yeah, whatever, I heard that same story so many
times that I don't paid the bull shit any mind. Any way,
what you do for a living?" Yanira asked me, drawing her
eyes together with concentration.

"A whole lot of nothing and a little bit of everything,"
I responded with a smile.

"Dat must be pretty interested," Yanira said with a
bitch-please-look on her face.

"Sometimes."

"Maybe I could hook you up with a spot in one of the
titty bars. I mean, you look way better than half of than
disease spreading whores who be dancing just to support
their pill addiction."

"What kinda pills those bitches be popping?"

"Oxycontin! It's a synthetic morphine for chronic pain or for the terminally ill. Some of those bitches be crushing them to snort it, some of them smoke, and some of the hard core tecatas, junkies inject it. That shit is called on the street, hillbilly heroin."

Bitch do I look stupid to you? I know what oxy is.

"How much an oxy pill goes for in the club?"

"Eighty dollars a pop! Why do you ask?"

"Young buck, today is your lucky day."

"Oh really!"

"Like I said earlier, act like you got some sense and you won't have to worry about eating, because I'm about to show you how to make some serious paper without you having to sell any more pussy. If you don't like what I'm saying to you, than bounce."

CHAPTER 13

"Heartless"

At the break of dawn, early the next day I was up and ready. Dressed in black from head to toe's, in some Paragueo jeans, a black Prada t-shirt, some black Prada sneakers, a black leather Prada jacket, and a pair of black Safilo's sunglasses, and for safety, I threw a black .50 caliber Desert Eagle handgun in my black Louis Vuitton hand bag. I decided to give Justice a break. I was dress for the occasion. It was gonna be a black muthafucking day for someone.

I stood on the corner of the pet Cemetery between 9th Street and Germantown Avenue where all the dope fiends, crack heads and street whores did their thing. As I stood in the center of the Badlands, reflection of my childhood had me in the trenches.

Broad daylight.

What a fucking amazing, unbelievable scene. All I could hear were has-been drug dealers hollering the name brand of their drug package, and whores walking up and down Germantown Avenue selling pussy and offering blow jobs for half price, five dollars, the price of a rock. The view on Germantown Avenue was spectacular, at any moment, without any warning, violent could strike.

I scanned the block over and over again, watching all the action; As much as I hated what I saw, I had to admit, these were my people, and they were making their cash the only way they knew how. They had no other option. I to tried sort through the chaotic scenery of the moment and get myself together, but I couldn't help but feel connected to the reality most of my people in North Philly were facing. Ninety percent of the people down Germantown Avenue had already been sentence to the death penalty of reality, to either die of Aids, over dose on drugs, or get shot in the head, and the other ten percent were on their way to the penitentiary to serve the remaining of their lives mopping floors, cleaning showers, fucking fagots in the ass, or washing pots and pan for eighteen-cents an hour.

Bitch don't go act soft on me. These assholes out here doing what they doing because they want. No one is forcing them to live like animals. They had the same opportunities you had, so fuck 'em! My conscious was talking mad shit to me. I had to remind myself that I didn't have the luxury to be catching feelings about the unpleasantly way of life in the Badlands.

My foster parent's house was completely dark, although it was broad daylight outside. My adrenalin was pumping fast. As always, my pussy hole feeling as it -was going through withdrawals from drugs addiction- the sweats, shakes, cramps in my gut, I knew I had to get me a fix. I be bullshitting y'all if I didn't tell you that I was addicted to spilling the blood of others.

Once I stepped into the living room a wall clock ticked in silence. The humming from the refrigerator echoed through the house. My eyes caught the shadow of a rat that peek its head from under the couch. Needless to say, the house smelled like shit and urine.

As I walked down the hallway, making my way to their bedroom, I grabbed an iron that was laying flat on top of a small glass table. My gut cramped. My pussy hole was leaking in a fast pace, damn! I slid open the bed room door and stepped into what was about to become a death chamber. I stood over the bed where the two greasy, scumbags, I hated the most were sprawled out, naked on their stomach. I plugged the iron into the extension-cord, turned the knob up to ten and waited for it to heat up. After five minutes I was ready to get my daily dose of death. I put on a pair of latex gloves, lifted the dirty sheets up from their body with the tip of my fingers, and pressed the hot iron flat on top of my adopted father ass cheeks. He screamed like a bitch a second later, but as quick as he began to scream I silence him, the cold metal on my black .50 caliber Desert Eagle was cracking him in his fucking mouth with such a powerful force, that every time I made contact a bloody tooth would fly out of his mouth. I split both of his lips in half.

"You fat, dirty, greasy bitch, don't move and don't scream, cause if you do, I swear, I will break your stinking ass the fuck up," I whispered. My adopted mother eyes widen, but she remained motionless.

I reached inside my jacket and pulled out a set of handcuffs, smacked my adopted mother in the face with them and order her to cuff my adopted father up. "Listen to me real clear, because I hate repeating myself. Cuff his right hand up to his left ankle and than do the same with his left hand and his right ankle. If you fuck up I will tear your face up." My adopted mother wasted no time in following my instruction. I was willing to bet that she was prepared to betray the love of her life just to save hers. Once he was in a crisscross position, I placed him on his back. I than order my adopted mother to lay on the bed, where I proceed to cuff her stinking ass up to the bedpost. *This shit was to easy. These two perverts didn't even try to fight.* I took a dirty ass shoe that had dry dog shit stuck on the bottom of it, and stuffed inside my adopted father mouth, as far as it would go. His busted lips stretched all the way till it appeared as if he was sporting four lips. Tears leaked from his eyes.

"You can't do this to us! We raise you! You're an ungrateful little whore," my adopted mother yelled.

"You dirty ass puerca, pig, you must be mistaking me for somebody who gives a fuck. You didn't raise me! You abused me, and treated me like a stepchild, now it's time to pay for your sins."

"Why? Who the fuck you think you are?"

"I'm the same little girl you allowed to be rape by your lovely husband here," I said, kicking my adopted father in the face three times. I was really trying to shovel the shoe in his mouth down his throat.

"But-"

"But my ass! Y'all two sick muthsfuckas are about to see a cold blooded, heartless bitch issue a little street justice," I said, plugging the iron back up. Shooting these two, uncivilized, pieces of shit would've been too easy. I wanted to be the last bitch they saw before I pushed their wig back, cause today was definitely their last day on this fucking earth.

Once the iron was hot again. I unplugged it and brought it close to my foster mother jelly stomach. I watched her face twisted in fear. Without a warning, I pressed the hot iron between her legs. The smell of dirty burnt pussy instantly penetrated the interior of the room. When I pulled the iron back, her pussy looked like melted gum. Skin was sticking to the iron, dripping as if it was wax from a candle.

I looked at my adopted father who was laying on his back with his asshole expose and his wrinkles nuts hanging lose. He nearly shivered at the contempt in my expression. No words needed to be spoken to know what I had in mind for this fool.

"Didn't I tell you that I was gonna come see you, if I found out that you was fucking Yanira. You're little father's game is up!"

"Please neña, girl! Don Rodriguez said, muffling the word please. When he felt the heat of the iron, he tried to spit the shoe out of his mouth. My blood chilled in my veins.

"You're in no position to be saying shit to me; you must pay for your sins, Papi! A taste of young pussy come with a price tag," I said, as I pressed the hot iron flat on his balls. Before he muster enough energy to scream, I shot him once in the temple, execution style. I then looked at my adopted mother and winked at her. She must've thought I was gonna spare her life, because she smile and said, "I won't tell anyone. Plus, he got what his hands called. I tried to tell him to leave them young girls along, but he wouldn't-"

"Bitch, stop lying," I replied, as I fire one shot to the side of her face, which blew a hole the side of a soft ball on her mug. If the city decides to give her a funeral, it would definitely be a close casket viewing.

CHAPTER 14
"Icing On The Cake"

Eight-forty-five the next morning I was parked in front of the storage Center on Delaware Avenue. I switched off the engine; and observed the manager.

Old man Billy Ray stood up. He scratched his filthy nut sack a few time before he grabbed the Styrofoam cup of coffee off the counter and brought it up to his mouth. I hunched over the wheel, and surveyed both sides of the street, in search of anything out of the ordinary.

I open my paragueo Jeans, pulled them down to my ankles, pushed my tongs to the side, and began to finger fuck my already wet pussy. Once I felt my juice flowing out of me, I blew out a hard breath as if I'd just been kicked in the stomach. Ever since I inherited Sweep Lips kidneys, my pussy hole stay leaking, before and after or while I'm in the process of pushing someone wig back. I wiggled my ass back into my jeans and got out my car, walking into the Storage Center with a *I-dare-you-muthafucka-to-say-the-wrong-shit-to-me-today, look.*

I immediately caught the attention of old man Billy Ray.

"Welcome back young lady. It's been a while since I last seen you round here. I even tried to contact you via-mail to inform you that your rental storage is due at the end of this month.

Shit! I'm slipping. How the fuck I could've forget! I got too much too lose. These rental storage centers will sale your storage space for a few hundreds dollars with everything in it if the rent is not paid on time. I might as well handle that shit now.

"Billy Ray, my mother passed away and I been stressed out about it, but now that I'm here, can I paid the rent for the next year?" I said reaching into my jacket pocket and pulling out a stack of one hundreds dollars bills, than added, "How much is to keep it paid for the whole year?"

Billy Ray licked his lips, and stared at me from head to toes. Men are all the same, low down dirty dogs. They see a nice piece of pussy and they automatic feel like they could get some. Billy Ray old ass was no different. I read right through him. Since I was feeling good, I decided to play head games with this old scum-bag just to see how far would he go.

"You know Billy Ray, I haven't been with a man in

years. I'm actually a dyke. Nevertheless, I'm willing to bet that you got a big, old, fat, dick." Billy Ray was all smiles. I looked down at his dick and the old man was already leaking.

"Well young lady, if you are interested in judging for yourself I be more than happy to show you my dick." Billy Ray was beyond himself. His eyes spoke a thousand stories, and his facial expression told me he wasn't gonna turn down no young pussy, I smiled.

"Billy Ray, I don't got all day, so are you gonna let me see you dick or not?" He stared at me and pulled his zipper down, whipping out a long black dick. I know in his younger days Billy Ray was getting plenty of pussy.

"Billy Ray, you packing something nice, but since I'm a dyke, I'm not impressed. However, since you are a nice old man, I'm gonna give you a good hand job, so pull your pants down." When Billy Ray pulled his pants down, I felt to the floor laughing, this old muthafucka was wearing a diaper. *I'ma have some fun with this asshole. I'ma make him regret the day he desired a piece of young pussy.* I took Justice out my jacket, and wrapped a piece of sandwich wrapper that was on the floor, around the barrel, and began jerking off Bill Ray. When I had him completely hard, I spitted on Justice and inserted the barrel into his anus. *I know this old scum-bag will need another diaper once I'm done with him.* By the time Billy Ray noticed what was going he was in another zone, shaking his ass like a bitch. It's amazing to see how easy a bitch could turn a nigga out without giving up the pussy.

Billy Ray looked at me and nodded. When he finally was able to say a word, he sounded as if his throat was dry. "Damn, young lady, what is you doing to this old man?"

"Nothing! You like it, right?"

"Hell yeah!"

Muthafucka, now it's time to stop. You're enjoying this shit little too much. Once I felt Billy Ray was ready to bust his nut, I let go of his dick, and' said, "You could finish yourself off, now do I still have to paid the full amount for the rent, or do I get a discount, Papi?"

"Girl, Billy Ray runs this place. You don't have to paid, I cover the bill myself."

"Listen carefully, Papi, I don't want no bullshit."

"Old man Billy Ray been working here, this job for thirty-five years. If I say I got you, believe me, I got you."

"That's all I want to hear." I winked at him as I walked into my storage space. I scanned the room carefully; making sure nothing was out of place. Two hundred boxes neatly stack against the wall. I separated the ecstasy pills from the Oxy. There were two hundred boxes of Oxy. Each box contained twenty zip-zag sandwich bags with two hundred Oxy pills in it, eighty-milligram. I quickly did the math in my head and the numbers were mind blowing. Sixteen thousand dollars for each zip-zag sandwich bag. *Damn, its on and popping! If what Yanira said to me earlier is truth, in a matter of days she will be the queen of oxycontin in the City.* I thought to myself as I grabbed five zip-zag bags of oxycontin and secured them inside Prada leather jacket. Shit, the city of Brotherly Love was about to witness the making of a heartless bitch, because I had every intention of turning Yanira into a ruthless muthafucka. Yeah, the city was about to be introduce to a new kind of beast.

Yo, somethings have to be discovered, not taught.

Yanira stared at the ceiling, more precisely at the expense art hanging on the walls. The last time she had a good night sleep, her life was turned upside down, and she was kicked out of her house butt-ass naked. So having a good night sleep without being sexually attacked or force to suck someone's dick was a refreshing welcoming. She kept closing her eyes, doing relaxation exercises, but her though kept returning to her mother and how she done her wrong. *How the fuck could she just do me like this? First chance I get dat nasty bitch is gonna pay for what she did to me. I'm sure we gonna bump heads again, mom!* She thought to herself as she turned over and pressed her face into the pillow.

I observed Yanira for a good half hour before, I decided to interrupt her comfortably mood. One thing she was gonna learn fucking with me, was that I rarely had time to sleep. In my line of work, you have to be ready to move out at any time of the day. So, if this bitch think she was just gonna lay her pretty ass down and sleep all day, she had something else coming.

"How'd you sleep?" I asked.

"Oh, shit! You scare the shit out of me. How long you been here?" Yanira asked sitting up on the bed.

"I just got here!" I lied.

"I slept like a baby."

I nodded, not sure if this was the right time for me to put my shit down. I couldn't afford the luxury of having this chick bounce on me, at least not now.

"Well get up, shower, and go in my room and help yourself to whatever you like in my closet. You and I are about the same size. I'm taking you shopping."

Yanira went into the shower and I disappeared into the living room. I was left with my own thoughts, which were going in one narrow direction. I wanted to call Detective Sandra Ortiz but I didn't want this pretty bitch to feel or think as if I was sweating her. Fuck it, let me text her just to see what kind of fish I can catch. I said to myself as I pulled out my cell phone from my bag and began texting her.

FYEO...For your eyes only. FWIW'..For what it's worth PCM...Please call me. LMAS...Lets meet again soon. IREOFNT...I really enjoyed our first night together. LMIHA...Let's make it happen again. TTYL...Talk to you later. HAND...Have a nice day.

IWSPN... I want some pussy, now. As soon as I pressed the sent button, Yanira walked into my living room looking like a model straight out of a Victoria secret catalog. I can't even front, baby girl was wearing my clothes as if they were hers. She was definitely dressing to impress.

"Amazing," I said when she stood in front, as if she was seeking my approval. Her lips curled into a smile.

"Thank you for allowing me to wear your clothes. We are almost the size."

My Gucci t-shirt couldn't hide the hard buds of her nipples. My Dolce and Gabbana jeans had her young pussy in a choke hold, and my high-heels, over the knee Prada boots had her looking like a high price call girl. Yanira was definitely a heart breaker. There was no doubt in my mind that she was gonna have a line of niggas trying to smash. Shit! If it wasn't because she was under age, I be licking her kitten.

"No problem. Are you ready?"

"As I'll ever be."

After hitting all the high end stores down center city, Yanira had twenty bags of new gear. She had Gucci, Prada, Fendi, Chanel, Versace, Moschino, Dolce and Gabbana, Stella McCartney. The little bitch probably couldn't pronounce half of the names in her shopping bag, but that meant nothing to me, because I needed to keep Yanira proper. She was my experiment, and by the time I was done with her, her name will be legendary. The way I saw it, the streets of Philadelphia only had room for one Queen Bee. Niggas and bitches were about to feel the effect of a heartless bitch. Jay-Z said it best, once a good girl gone bad, there is not turning back. Once Yanira got a taste of the glamorous life, I was about to introduce her dumb ass to, the bitch will kill God if I asked her to do so. Ain't no broke bitch gonna turn down unlimited shopping sprees, unlimited funds, new cars, and lavish living without haven't to fuck. I ain't doing nothing a nigga don't do when he trying to lock some young pussy down. I consider myself a female pimp; therefore, I must keep my top whore laced up looking like a million bucks. Yanira was no difference from any other dumb hood rat bitch. Her life story was great fiction. She needed a hero in her life, and I just happen to be at the right place at the right time.

On the drive back to my apartment, Yanira smiled from ear to ear. Never in her young life has she been treated to such a shopping spree.

"Yanira when do you turn eighteen?" I asked her, making plans in my head to turn her ass out of some pussy, on her birthday. I wasn't gonna stand around and allow no young nut to benefit from what I was building, nah! Fuck that!

"I turn eighteen on October 25, 2010," she replied with curious eye, than added, "why do you care?"

"I want to know the real you," I said.

"Come on sis', we both from the hood, keep it one hundred with me." Dis bitch don't think I noticed how she be looking at me. *She don't think I know she's a dyke. The bitch is too smart for herself. Bitch! I notice the bag of sexual toys in your closet. But if playing dumb was going to get me where I wanted to be, so be it. Inez, Jasmine, whatever dis bitch call herself, is the kind of bitch who always want to be in control of things. She the kind of bitch who, needs to keep a low self-esteem bitch next to her, which enable her to feel good about herself.* Yanira thought as she smiled from ear to ear.

"Yanira, you know them others chicken-head, disease spreading ho's at the titty bar you work in, are going to be green with envy when they see you with your new gear on."

"Club Onyx is not a titty bar. It's an up-scale spot for the working professional," Yanira responded with an attitude.

I unzipped my Gucci bag and pulled a zip-zag bag of Oxy and laid it on her lap, and then added, "Are you ready to take your hustling game to the next level or what?"

Yanira eyes widen. *This was the meal ticket, I been searching for. This was my chance to shine on my own, to break away from all than others chickens-head who had to sell pussy to make it through the day. If I blow it, I doubted I get another chance. If I succeed, I could tell all those scum-bags who done me wrong to kiss my ass.* Yanira thought to herself as her eyebrows went up, "Wow!"

"What does that mean?" I asked, playing dumb.

"It means that this is a once in a life time opportunity. Yo! I could sale these in one night, trust me!" Yanira grabbed the bag of Oxy in her hands and study it for a long while.

"Fantastic! When do we begin?"

"Today! Now!" Yanira was excited.

"Really?"

"Yeah! We might as well get this money now. Do you know where Club Onxy is at?"

"Down Delaware Avenue, right?" I responded, observing my new recruit bask in the joy of her new come up. Only if she knew that everything that shine ain't gold. But at this moment, this shit was icing on the cake for me.

CHAPTER 15
"In The Club"

Club Onyx...

Every city has a hot spot where the working class can congregate at. In Philadelphia its club Qnxy. This professional hangout has an infamous reputation for attracting, under cover cop's, security guards, mail men's and correctional officers from New Jersey, Wilmington, DE, and of course, Philly.

This was the spot were cold blooded whore came to drain the pockets of the working niggas who think their shit don't stink.

Club Onxy was a safe heaven for wannabe players who wore fake jewelry, front like they ware sitting on some major paper. These fake ass players would roll up in the club and stroke the ego of them broke ass strippers, just to get some ass. Most of the strippers in Club Onxy were drug addicts, dancing to support their habit. On certain nights, Club Onxy feature Correctional officers from CFCF and Graterford prison, and today, was one of those nights. These dirty ass, Avon wearing prison guards were ex-welfare recipient who been force off welfare and force to find themselves a job. Being though the prison system doesn't give a fuck about who they hire, they target the strip clubs in Philly as a recruiting ground. As a result of it, they end up with a pool of recruits that can't even spill their own name. In some cases, the only requirement to be a correctional officer is to be able to turn a key and look up a nigga ass, oh, and not have a felony.

The strippers who take jobs as prison guards always bring the stripper mentality with them. Most of them bitches ain't shit but low budget dick eaters.

The rules in Club Onxy were the same rules most of them whore pick up in prison. Get money, get you're freak on anything goes.

Once we enter the club, one of the bouncer helped himself to a handful of Yanira heart shape, ass.

"Damn baby girl, you gotta be the finest thing up in this place tonight. Shit! I could really use a piece of pussy right now. What you say if we go into the bathroom and do a quickie," the bouncer pulled out a condom, Lambskin, tearing the foil package open with his teeth.

I had trouble keeping my excitement from showing. Yanira was holding her own like a true pro. *I knew it! I knew it! I knew It! I knew this little bitch I was into something heavy other than dancing.* A few of the strippers walked by and slowed down to look at Yanira. I found myself enjoying the attention she was getting. Up until this moment I'd imagine that Yanira was a victim, but now I wonder whether it had all been an illusion. *Could this young bitch be running game on me? Nah! She ain't that sharp.*

"Chill big homie, I'm with my sister, but I promise you that tomorrow I will spend the whole night with you."

"You're promise?"

"When have I ever sold you a dream? Can't no nigga tap this ass the way you do," "Yanira said, as the bouncer pinched her nipples. I kept my eyes fixed on her. When Yanira walked over to me she whispered in my ear, "He's just a nut ass nigga who been trying to get me to suck his dick. He's the head bouncer of security of the club."

"Baby girl, you don't have to convince me of anything. Plus, it pays off to have friends in all walks of life," I said acting as if I didn't noticed the Lambskin in ol' boys hand.

I was trying not to be so obvious about being in the club, but every few steps some nigga would stop me and Yanira and say something like, "'My heavens! How much for a lap dance?" Others were blunt about their desires and would, straight up said, "How much for the whole package?" One ugly, fat Joe, wanna be, Puerto Rican nigga, just walked behind Yanira and I, pulled out his cell phone, and snapped a picture of our asses. One midget with a big ass head, copped himself a free feel. I was about to kick him in the face, but I felt sorry for him when I looked down on him. Instead I smiled and demand that he keep me company for the night.

"Listen here you're big head muthafucka, since you like to touch without asking, I should just jump on your ass. But since you're kind of cute, I tell you what, you could either rock out and hang with me for the night, or take an ass whipping for touching me? So what it's gonna be?"

Yanira died laughing when she saw the midget grabbed on to my leg like a lost kid, and say, "I'll hang out with you tonight," The midget said, than added, "*By the way, my name Kelvin Mosantos, but everyone calls me Nino." Nino the midget was riding on cloud nine. I could see the hate in the others wanna be players, when they saw him walking with me towards the bar. For a second I couldn't believe what I was witnessing.

On top of the bar there was a Dominican chick, squatting over a bottle of Gray Goose, slowing inserting it into her pussy. All the horny ass working niggas and freak bitches alike went bananas. Half drunk niggas began throwing dollar bills on top of the Dominican chick who was now laying on her back with the bottle of Gray Goose half way inside of her.

"Which one of your players is trying to drink some special Gray Goose" The D.J., hollered into the mic, as the Dominican chick slowly withdrawal the bottle out of her wet pussy. The crowd went crazy as Lusty, the Dominican chick stood up and made her ass cheeks claps. The whole place was in awe. Money was raining on top of Lusty.

'Which one of y'all ballers want an up, close and personal with Lusty?" The DJ hollered again, over the mic. Niggas were screaming the from top of their lungs, "How Much?"

One pretender held his right hand up, exposing ten one hundred dollars bills, "Come to Papi," he yelled as he reached out for Lusty, sliding a crispy one hundred dollar bill into her pussy.

"Damn nigga, you fucking the game up!" Another great pretender, half drunk, nigga screamed, putting away his handful of one dollar bills.

"Dis ain't for pretenders. Dis is for real niggas with money to spend!" The chump with the thousand said, as he stoops up trying to feel Lusty pussy again.

"That's a nasty ho!" The Nino the midget said to me as he reached into his pocket and pulled out his cell phone.

"How would you know?" I asked him.

"Look, I gotta handle some business, I catch up with you in a while. So I leave you're two love birds together, so you could get to know each other," Yanira said, as she walked away with a smile.

"Now back to you, Nino, what are you about to do with that cell phone?"

"I'm about to document this shit in here. You see, half

of these niggas up here, trying to feel that whore pussy, are fronting. They pop up in here spending their money, but half of them suppose to be these respectable muthafuckas, who be trying to impose their bullshit morality on the rest of us. You see that nigga up there, the one standing next to the great pretender," Nino said, pointing to a well dressed black man, who looked like he was out of place. "He's the president of the City council by day, but by night, he be up in these strip clubs tricking. That whore Lusty be fucking for pennies. She had a partner who use to be queen whore of the Philadelphia police department, but for the last year, Lusty been up in here by herself. Believe it or not, Lusty is a correctional officer up in Graterford prison. She be acting like she law and order. My sources tell me she fucks with them white guards for money." I sat there and listen to Nino the midget run his mouth. This nigga only had one drink up in him, and he was spilling his gust out to me, I could just imagine if he was completely drunk.

"Nino, what you do for a living?" I asked, he seems to be on an emotional matrix. This big head midget appeared to be in desperate need of a savior.

"I'm an attorney! I represent the high rollers in the city. My retaining fee start at twenty thousand. Why do you think, I love coming up in these clubs, because I collect footage of some of the decision makers in the city. When I call in a favor, I get it. When I walk into a courtroom in this city, I always win. Most of my cases are won before I even go to court. Justice is not about right or wrong, it's about who you know. If you ever need a lawyer give me a call," Nino said, as he reached into his pocket and pulled out four business cards. "Here, my home number is on the back." Nino and I sat at the far end of the bar and talked about everything. I was impressed with all the information he voluntarily was giving me. At that moment, I made the decision to keep Nino the midget as a friend. I'm sure he could come in handy later on down the line.

"Thanks you for the cards, I'll definitely will keep your number in mind. Now order me a Long Island iced tea." I needed to stay focus on Yanira, so I wasn't about to indulge in any heavy drinking.

When the clown with the thousand dollars was right under Lusty ass, she bent over and Gray Goose came spraying out of her pussy, onto his face. The whole club went crazy.

"What's up mama? How much for a shot?" one brother asked while trying to cop himself a free feel.

"Listen here player, I'm here with my man. He might be short, but he can handle his own. So go on with your bullshit, it ain't that kind of party. Trust me, you don't want me to cut my pit-bull loose," I said, looking down at Nino the midget, hoping he wouldn't chump himself, because from the way the drunk nigga in front of us was acting, a beat down was unavoidable.

"Bitch! You ain't special! You up in here dick teasing

a nigga, talking dat dumb shit, about it ain't dat kind of party! Fuck outta here. Fuck you and dat little-"

Before the drunk was able to finish what he wanted to express, Nino the midget punched him straight in his nuts. The drunk fell to the floor like a bag of shit.

"Nigga, I may be small in stature but I will fuck you up! Don't ever disrespect my woman again." Nino the midget said. The bouncer, who approached Yanira when we first arrived at the club, picked the drunk up and dragged him out the club.

"Excuse me-"

"Nigga didn't I just told you it wasn't that kind of party!" I said, turning around to show whoever the voice belong to how grimy a bitch can get.

"Damn baby, calm down."

"How did you know I was here? By the way, meet my little man, his name is Nino

"I know you from somewhere! Anyway, my name is Sandra." Detective Orttz said, looking at Nino as if she was trying to remember where she knew him from. She then directed her attention back to me. My heart skipped a beat when she bent over and rubbed her tongue between my cleavages.

"I just walked in and saw the show your little man was putting on, and I was surprise to see you in the middle of it. I did receive your text massage."

I leaned over, so my mouth was very close to her ear.

I was so close, she could feel my warm breath, "You know tonight you gonna have to let me hit that pussy."

"What about your little man here?" Ortiz said staring down at Nino who was enjoying the conversation.

"We could either have a threesome with him, or I could get with you tomorrow." I included Nino the midget because I knew Ortiz wasn't gonna turn my proposition down.

"Shit! I never been with a midget before. I guess there's a first time for everything. By the way, I want you to pull my hair and smack my ass," Detective Ortiz said, pulling the zipper of my jeans down, sliding three fingers into my pussy, massaging my clitoris.

"Uhhmm, I'm about to come," I said, coming all over Detective Ortiz hand. She pulled her fingers from out my pussy, and stuck them inside of Nino mouth, "Don't she taste good?" Nino's reaction was all that was needed to confirm his answer. He began licking Ortiz fingers one by one.

"You ain't seen nothing yet," Ortiz whispered in a soft voice.

"What a small world, huh?" A man voice said, as he placed his hand on my shoulders.

Man not again! Who the fuck is this nigga? I'm really ain't trying to knock another nigga out. Nino the midget thought to himself as he stepped back to observe what he consider, strip club drama.

"Nigga, do I know you?"

"Bitch, don't make me act stupid up in dis mutha-fucka."

"Bitch ass nigga, you got about ten seconds to get your trifling hands off me, cause I'm the one who gonna act stupid up in this place."

The clown that got sprayed with Gray Goose by the dirty, Dominican, looking chick was on some bullshit, getting ready to fuck up the vibe in the club.

"What da fuck you do with my baby? I should just whip your ass on G.P. What da fuck you did to my baby? I'm not gonna keep asking you."

"For the last time! I don't know you! I never seen you in my life, so get the fuck outta my face, before shit get ugly for you." I was about to bang this clown brains out if he kept annoying me with his baby drama bullshit.

"Mita, Sweep Lip's, whatever da fuck you call yourself. Don't act like you don't know who da fuck I be! I'm the same nigga who fucked you in the ass! You know, who the fuck I am!"

This clown got me confused with Sweet Lips. Damn, that bitch was double dipping. Pregnant! I be damn! I thought to myself as I stared at him in shock. The last encounter I had with Sweet Lips she was claiming to be pregnant. Not only did I possibly killed my biological mother, but I also killed a brother or sister, shit!

"Let me talk to you outside, player," I said, looking

around, making sure this clown wasn't drawing too much attention. I was ready to put this nigga lights out.

"Nah ho! We gonna talk, here and now!"

"Hold up William, you got the wrong person," Detective Ortiz said, sliding in between William and I.

"You know this clown!?" I asked with a serious face.

"Yeah! Yeah! He's a friend.

"A friend! Bitch, was I a friend when you was sucking my dick? Na mean!" William said, reaching into his jacket pocket, but before he was able to pull his hands back out, I had my .50 caliber place directly under his nuts.

"Nigga, you got two options, you could either die here with your nuts all over this place, or you could take your drunk ass out of here, alive, while you still got a chance." I said with much larceny in my heart. Detective Ortiz laughed, which caused William to become enrage even more.

"Fuck you, Sandra, you pussy-eating dyke, freak."

"I may be a dyke, but at least I'm not out here acting a fool, letting some nasty whore urinate all over my face. Take my advice; get the fuck out of here before you end up without balls. Oh, by the way, I'm willing to bet, little man here can handle the pussy better than you, asshole," Ortiz said, adding salt to the injuries. Nino, laughed, which caused William to charge towards him, but before he was able to get his hands around Nino the midget neck, the bouncer put his dumb ass in a choke hold.

"Nigga, I will crush your windpipe if you act crazy again. I 'ma let you go, but you better be easy."

"I don't want no trouble! I see y'all two whores around," William said, leaving the club feeling like a cold blooded pussy. He couldn't believe he got chump by two bitches, and put in a choke hold at the same time. *"I take the L for now!"* William thought to himself as he stumble to the floor next to his car in the parking lot of the club.

"What the fuck that nigga was tripping about?" I asked Detective Ortiz, who was still smiling as if she was watching a comedy show.

"He been acting funny ever since his baby momma did a disappearing act on him. He musta thought you was her."

"That nasty shit that chicken head sprayed on him must've have him going crazy, that nigga got a lot of hostility inside of him." Suddenly I felt someone tap me the shoulders. I rose and turned, thinking I would be confronting the drunken asshole who was testing my patient again. However, Yanira was staring at me with a big grin on her face.

"What's going on here?" She asked, looking at Detective Ortiz as if she was crazy, then at the midget, with a smile, shooting me facial expression that indicated to me that she has accomplish what she'd came to the club for.

"Sandra, Nino, this is my little sister, Yanira," I said, looking Yanira in the eyes.

"I'm ready to bounce, so can you take me home?" Yanira said while sipping on a glass of Martell on the rock, with her face frowned up.

I turned towards Detective Ortiz and whispered in her ear, "Listen, take little man over your place, and wait on me. I be there in about half hour. I'ma just drop my sister off at the house."

"Don't keep me waiting!" Detective Ortiz said, as she grabbed Nino the midget by the hand, and walked out the club under the watchful eyes of a bunch of hating pretenders, who were trying to figure out what Nino, the midget had that they didn't. "That's some gangsterish shit! That big head midget about to get his fuck on." One bystander said, shaking his head.

Twenty Minutes Later...

It was one forty in the morning when Yanira and I arrived at my apartment.

"Girl, I sold every last one of those pills," Yanira said with enthusiasm.

"How much did we made?" I asked her playing stupid. I wanted to see if she was gonna play me for a chump or get greedy on me.

"We made about eighteen thousands, cause some niggas just were dropping hundred dollar bills." Yanira opened a brown paper bag and poured the money on top of the glass table in the living room, than added, "I can't front, I never seen dis much paper in my life."

"Guess what, baby girl?"

"What?"

"You sea all that paper there! It's yours! Spent it on whatever you want to. Just make sure you save some for a rainy day.

"But-"

"Look at it this way, if you decide to work for me after tonight, I will give you half of everything we make. If you cross me, I will put a slug in your spinal cord."

"I'm loyal to those who are loyal to me. I might be young, but I never been a sneaky bitch. If I was gonna cross you I would've done it in the club."

"Baby girl, I'm just giving you the rules to my game. Time would tell, enjoy your money. I'll holler at you in the morning, I got to go handle some personal business."

"Anything I could help in?" Yanira asked me in a sexy voice.

Young buck, you're about to be eighteen in a few weeks! Trust me, when the time is right you will become very helpful to me. I thought as I walked out my apartment with a wet pussy.

I couldn't wait to get to Detective Ortiz house.

I want Yanira to think about my offer. I wanted her to see that I trusted her, by herself in my apartment. I was testing her, to see if she would snoop around. On purpose,

I left the remaining four zip-zag bags of Oxy pills on top of my bed. If she passes the test, she would definitely be my side kick whore.

If she fails, than she just be another potentially spent life in the streets of Philly. I already knew she wasn't afraid to hustle, but would she have the heart to exterminate someone from the face of this earth?

Give a bitch a strip pole, she's rich for a day, but teach that same bitch how to make love to a nigga or bitch mind, well, then, she's got something for the rest of her life, don't she?

Detective Sandra Ortiz House...

When I arrived at Sandra's house she was seated at the table waiting for me butt-ass naked, while Nino the midget was fully clothed.

"Girl what took you so long..." Sandra began, "I'm horny as hell. I was about to-"

"You should of give my little man some of that good pussy. I'm' sure he would've been grateful."

"But I wanted you here to be part of this threesome." I totally ignored her remarks. *This dumb bitch was about to find out who was really in-charge*

"Listen, here you're big head muthafucka, you may as well know that, I have very strict terms about who I fuck. I don't share pussy! You gonna have to pick which one of us you want to fuck. And as soon as you're done busting your nut, you got to bounce. "Now make your pick."

It took Nino the midget a moment to pick. Although Ortiz was nothing but pure eye candy, Nino the midget selected me. I was delighted. I haven't had dick in so long that I had forgotten what dick looked like.

"Get undressed," I hissed. "Then... let's fuck!"

Nino quickly took off his cloths. I stared open-mouthed at his dick, unable to compare it to the rest of his body. This big head midget was packing a dick of a normal size nigga. He was packing at least nine inches. I could see the hate in Ortiz eyes.

"Okay, babe, let me show you what this big head midget could do," he growled, as he followed Ortiz and I into her bedroom. As soon as I was on my back on the bed, I spread my legs invitingly, giving Nino the midget a tantalizing view straight up my pussy. He stared at my pink gash and partially opened pussy as if he was scare.

"Put in it into meeeeeee! You big head muthafacka." Without any preliminaries, the midget took his hard dick in his little hand, and guided it straight towards my wet, waiting pussy. He thrust himself down into my warm pussy tissues. I squeezed him with my pussy lips. I moved my hips in slow circles, giving him the best shot of pussy he aver had.

Our bodies ware moving together beautifully. At first

I'd took his gentleness as him being scare, but now I was beginning to understand that it was just his natural grace-his technique.

This fucking midget knew what he was doing and was doing it well.

"Damn! You have the tightest pussy I ever been in, I love it. I bet you never thought I could handle your pussy, huh?" he asked me, while popping one of my nipples into his mouth.

From the corner of my eyes I seen Ortiz climb on the bed behind the midget.

"Mmmmmmmmm. You feel so good!" My body began to sweat. My head felt like it was being charged up electrically. I felt the orgasm building inside of me. My pussy flashed with heat and friction. My spasms were severe, and caused my muscles to tighten dramatically around Nino the midget dick.

"Ooooooo damn, girl, yesss, baby," he let out when he felt Ortiz wet lips on his balls. His face distorted with pleasure.

"Yeah! suck my balls. I'ma bout-" I quickly pushed Nino the midget off me and let him spray his nut all over my stomach, while Ortiz licked it off.

"Well you big head nigga, it's time for you to bounce!"

"But, can I at least wash up?"

"Yeah! But not here! I'll call you tomorrow."

Nino put his cloths back on, and walked out of

Detective Ortiz house with a smile on his face. I looked at Ortiz and winked, which only caused her to become angry.

"That was some selfish bullshit you pulled. How the fuck you just gonna fuck a nigga in my house, in my bed, and not allow me to get any dick? You got this game twisted!"

"Nah, bitch, you got the game twisted! I'm about to show your ass who wear the pants in this house." Sexual excitement zinged through the room like electricity. Ortiz cast a nervous glance in my direction, wondering what I would do next.

Of course, she was furious, but I wasn't concerned about it. She tried to pretend like she didn't feel hurt by my comment. *Some bitches just deserve to be dogged. This bitch probably thought she had me by a string like a puppet cause I allowed her to take charge the first night. She's about to find out that I have no kindness toward her.*

CHAPTER 16

"Let's Get It On"

"Yes Mami, I want you to put a dent in my uterus."

"Whose pussy is this?"

"It's yours!"

"Say it in Spanish! Say it, Puta!"

"I said it belong to you! It hurt so good!"

"Bitch I can't hear you! Scream that shit. I want your neighbors to know who pussy is this. I'm gonna make sure you don't get no dick for at least a month."

"You hurting me!"

"A long dick suppose to hurt." Detective Ortiz screamed so loud that tears came out of her eyes.

She was lying sideways pressing her face into a pillow, as I slammed into her pussy. She had her left leg over mines. All twelve inches of my Puerto Rican dick was up in her. I was trying to inflect, upon her as much pain as possible. Once her juices started dripping down her inner thigh, I pulled all the way out of her, love tunnel, and let the crown of my dick rest on her clit.

"Ohhh, baby, please don't do this to me," Detective Ortiz needed to feel me inside of her.

"Calm down baby, you got me all night, but you gonna have to earn me! I wanna know where I could find your friend from the club the clown that fronted on me. I need to talk to him about his baby momma," I said, as I lifted her perfectly round 36DD into my mouth, sucking on the nipples, softly. I then slammed into her hard. She responded by throwing her heart shape ass back at me. I pulled her hair, and slid two fingers into her tight asshole.

"Shit! He lives with his mother down Master Street, on the blue corner house... Damn! Pull my hair a little harder." Detective Ortiz was exploding with multiple orgasms.

"Turn your ass over on your stomach and spread your legs!" When she had her ass cheeks spread open, I began to slide my long dick into her asshole.

"Take it easy. It hurt!"

"Bitch, stop fucking whining!" I smacked her hard on her ass cheeks, leaving my finger prints mark. "A little pain is nothing to a big whore like you," I said, reaching between her legs, massaging her clitoris.

"Let me ride you," Detective Ortiz requested, as I

pulled out of her ass. She then took a wet rag and wiped down my dick. She wasted no time in getting on top of me cowboy style, with her ass facing me.

"Uhhmm, I'm coming, again," her body shivered. When she finished coming, she laid her head on my chest. Typical women shit. *After a good fuck, they always want to have a pillow talk session.*

I laid back comfortably on her bed, watching re-runs of the Wendy Williams show. Suddenly, Detective Ortiz wanted to confess her sins to me.

"You know, I feel like our relationship is starting to get serious, so I want to share some of the personal things happening in my life. In our line of work, we never know what may happen when we walk out that door in the morning."

Bitch is you crazy? Serious relationship! We only been together twice, and you already talking about relationship! You're pathetic. I made sure I made a mental note of her words.

"I hear you, but what are you really saying? Cause I don't have a clue-"

"I was informed today, that the internal affairs and the District Attorney's office have me under investigation for corruption. They claim to have a snitch who's' saying that I been shaking down drug dealers. I'm just saying-"

"What are you saying? What does that have to do with me?"

"Nothing, really, but-"

"But what?" I said, clearing my throat.

"I just don't want you to hear it from some other source," Detective Ortiz replied. She stared at me trying to decided whether or not to go on. At the moment I realized that she was a soft bitch, with no confident. She looked live a powerless child.

"Listen here bitch, my only, my only concern in here, is pussy and pleasure! I'm not in the mood for a heart to hear. Not right now!"

She did not have an answer. She shook her head as if she couldn't believe what I was saying. "But I thought you cared about me?" She asked, her eyes getting all watery.

I got up from bed and took off my twelve inch strap on dildo, and smacked her on the side of her mouth with it. "All Philly cops are dirty. Welcome to the club! Maybe now you could sleep with a clear conscience mind," I said, as I got dress, with a devilish grin on my face.

"But I could go to prison for this!"

"You're talking to the wrong person. You need to go see Dr. Phil or someone who cares. Play the shit for what is worth! If I was you, I lawyer the fuck up! I get back to you another day."

"Do you know any good lawyer?" Were the last words I heard Detective Ortiz said as I walked out of her room, leaving her soft ass laying in her bed. This bitch had to lean the hard way that you make your bed, you lie and die in it. I left her house ready to raise hell. *Yeah I got a lawyer for you bitch, and his name is Nino "The midget" Mosantos.*

CHAPTER 17
"Karma Is A Muthafucka"

I flicked my Newport cigarette out the window when I saw the chubby, dark skinned Latina walking into the two story, brick house. I looked around, to ensure the coast down Master Street was clear.

Once inside Angelita put her Gucci bag down and headed upstairs to her bedroom to change. She went over to her drawer and pulled out a Victoria secrete Teddy set. She wanted to look sexy and prepare for the arrival of her young boy. Even at the age of fifty-four, Angelita still had a body most young girls could only dream of. When she bent over to put her tongs on, she felt the cold metal of a gun against the back of her head. Her eyes widen with fear, her breath suddenly was coming in heaves.

"Holy shit!" Angelita screamed out as she saw her whole life flash right in front of her.

"We could do this the easy way or the hard way. So your fat ass better decide real quick, because I' ma grimy bitch with little patience."

"What the hell you doing up in my house? Scant!"

"You are about to find out in a minute," I responded with a disparaging sound in the back of my throat. I pulled out a set of blindfold from my back pocket and placed them over her eyes. I wanted my subject in total darkness. Once I had her blindfold and handcuffed, I sat her fat ass down on a chair and duck taped her to it.

"Oh God! Oh sweet Jesus, help me!" Whimpered Angelita.

"Don't be asking God for help! Not after the trifling life your son lived."

Bitch ass nigga got his female tendencies from his momma.

"Go to hell, bitch!"

"Where the fuck is your son William at?"

Angelita lip tremble a bit, she imagine that this was about one of her son's. Until this moment, she lived a fairly ordinary life. She a was cougar who prided herself in turning young boys out, and as of now, like it or not, she was part of her son life.

"I don't know where my son is at. He got his own life and I got mines."

"Well guess what? Since you gave birth to him, and since you want to act all hard and shit, then you gonna suffer the consequences for his dirty deeds."

"What do you mean? I don't even know you!" She manage to say.

"I'm giving you one last chance to talk; do you know where I can find your son at? Do you have his cell phone number? I just want you to give me his number:"

Dis cabrona, bitch must think I'm crazy. If I reveal any information about my children's she gonna kill me anyway. I been around the block more than a few times to know what dis derange bitch had planned, Angelita was hoping for a miracle.

"Like I stated," my son has his own life.""

"I see we having a serious misunderstanding here, like maybe you're not understanding me or I'm not making myself clear. Just so that you don't get it twisted, let me lay it out for you, bitch! If you don't stop playing stupid with me, I'll blow your brains out. I will go to your daughter house and shoot her, your grandbabies, and anybody who gets in my path. Trust me, I'm not interested in Julie, Fred, Eric or you. I just want your son William. Losing one out of four ain't bad." Angelita didn't answer me. She just nodded her head, which only enraged me more.

Okay, let's play your game. Let's see how long your ass gonna be able to handle the pain. I said to myself as I picked up a hammer from my duffel bag. I also took out a raw potato and stuffed it into her mouth, then taped it shut. A second later, I slammed the hammer down on top of her big toenails, crushing it into a million little pieces of flesh and bone fragments.

"In case you don't know, ice water runs through my veins," I whispered in her ear in a rasp voice.

"Huh!"

"Huh my ass! I tried to be civilize about this shit, but you want to act stupid," I said, Angelita ayes flashed with a private pain that made my pussy hole itch with desire. I took the potato out of her mouth. I love to hear a person beg for mercy right before their about to die.

"Wait!"

"Now you want to cooperate! Nut is you crazy?" I said ominously.

"I tell you where you can find my son!"

This nut ass bitch don't understand what's going on here! I know she don't think I I'ma go for the okie-doke-shit. How the fuck she thinks she's gonna try to put me on a wild-goose chase! I should just show her how grimy I can get. I thought to myself as I shot her a I-don't-give-a-fuck-about-what-you-gota-say-to-me-look.

"It's too late for that baby." I placed the potato back into her mouth and a pillow over her face, then I jammed Justice into the center of the pillow. I wanted her to feel Justice and realize that the pillow would serve as a crude silence. Tears streamed down her cheeks. I wasn't move. I looked up towards the ceiling as if I was looking towards the sky and whispered, "This one is for you, Sweet Lip." I squeezed the trigger, emptying the whole clip into the pillow. Angelita head felt forward, towards her chest. Some people take the saying, blood is thicker than water to a whole new level, even if they gotta give up their life. This silly bitch could've prevented her own demise if she would've tell me where to find her bitch ass son. But nah, she wanted to be loyal, so she got her wig pushed back. As I pulled the blindfolds off of Angelita, I heard a loud knock on the front door. *Damn! Why some muthafuckas always got to show up at the wrong time?* I asked myself as I peeked out the bedroom window.

The big bold headed muthafucka was standing at the door steps with a cool-Aid smile. *I seen this nigga before! Hell nah! It can't be. This is the same nigga who laying pipe down on Diego wife. What the fuck is he doing here? I got a bad feeling about this.*

Knock! Knock! Knock! Knock! The banging on the door kept getting louder. I wanted to see if he was gonna leave, but instead, he pulled out his cell phone and started dialing a number. Three seconds later, the phone on top of Angelita dresser stared ringing.

Ring!...Ring!...Ring!...Ring!....

This maybe a set up! Should I pick it up? If I don't it may create a fed flag. Fuck it! I picked up the phone and a powerful male voice came through.

"Bitch, don't you hear me knocking on the door? What the fuck are you doing? Come down here and open it. Big dick daddy waiting on you-"

Hold up, player! I don't know what type of drugs you on, but you talking to the wrong person."

"Really?"

"Yeah, really! Now, who do you wish to talk to?" My voice was breathy low and seductive. I'm sure the tone of my voice was giving an erection to whoever this nigga was.

"I want to speak to Hot Stuff! Tell her big daddy Brown is here."

"She's ain't here!"

"What you mean, she ain't there? I just spoke to her a little while ago."

"What part of she ain't here don't you understand?"

"Dig this shorty, you got a slick mouth on you. I'm not the one you want to fuck with now, where Hot Stuff at?"

"First of all, I can back up whatever comes out my mouth, and second, Hot Stuff had an emergency."

"She didn't mention nothing about an emergency when we spoke."

"Well shit happen! If you want, you can wait for her. I'm sure she be back soon!"

"Bet! I do that! Are you gonna let me in the house?"

"Let me think about it. I don't let strangers in my crib."

"I'm not a stranger. I'm a friend of the family."

"Nigga, to me you're a stranger, as far I'm, concern,

you might be the North Philly strangler."

"Shorty, are you kidding me?" I didn't even responded. I made his ass wait five minutes before I let him into the house.

"Shorty, you're outa you're fucking mind, but you're fine as hell. What's your name?"

"Juicy Lips." I replied.

"Are they really juicy, or is that just your nick name?" Captain Brown said, rubbing his beard. His dick got harder than a still pole. I walked up to him and graded it.

"Is it true what they said, that black man got big dicks?"

"I could show you better than I could 'tell you." Captain Brown unzipped his pants down, whipping out his long dick.

"I let you guess for yourself!"

"I feel you player!" I smiled because niggas always think a bitch is impress by a big dick. Most big dick niggas don't even know how to rock a bitch world. Plus, the majority of women's out here don't really want a big dick nigga tearing their inside up.

Most bisexual lesbians rather have a medium size, seven to eight inch. Medium size dick niggas stand a better chance of getting some back door action, or getting deep throat. Captain Brown was about to be introduced to the cruel reality of a bitch who really don't give a fuck about no dick.

"Drop them panties, shorty! So I could show you what I could do with this animal," Captain Brown pulled on his dick, making the crown pop out.

"Not here. I respect my mom's crib. But we can go somewhere where we can enjoy each other."

"What hotel do you wanna go to?" He asked, hoping it wasn't an expensive one. But I had other plans for him.

"We don't have to go to no hotel! Why spend your hard earning money, when I got my own crib a few blocks from here. We can get our freak on without any interruption."

"Can I at least get a lil' head?" He asked me, pinching my hard nipples through my shirt.

"I rather wait! Be easy. Once we get to my crib you can' get the whole package, so lets bounce." I said, leading the way out the house. I was dying to get out of there before someone else popped up.

"We walking?" He asked.

"Yeah! I don't a have a car- it's in the shop."

I'm not walking down this neighborhood in this correctional officer uniform. We could drive in my car," he said, as he opened the door of a blue Jaguar.

"Don't tell me you one of those scary ass nigga." I was feeling him out, but it was clear that the only thing on his mind was pussy.

Hell naw! I'm all hood baby. I just don't want niggas to get the wrong impression. Where do you live at.

"2345 North 6ᵗʰ street!" Captain Brown hit the gas paddle then turned right on German town Avenue, onto Indiana Avenue on a one way street.

"Yo! This is a one way street," I said, looking him straight in his eyes.

"I know, but it's the shortest way to your crib. Ain't no police down here anyway," he replied, as he placed his right hand on my knees, trying to slide it down my pant.

"Chill nigga! I rather wait for the real thing. What the fuck can your finger do to me? I'm a grown ass woman with a desire for big dicks."

"You really gonna make a nigga wait, huh, shorty?"

"Why not? Plus, I don't want your uniform to get all messy, your wife might noticed."

"I ain't got no wife! Too much pussy out here for a nigga to be on lock. How about you, do you have a man?"

"Does it matter? I'm a freak, I fuck whoever I want to fuck, can't you tell?"

Once we pulled up in front of Diego house, Captain Brown eyes widen, almost as if he couldn't believe what he was seeing.

"You live there?" He asked, pointing towards the house he been in on more than a few occasions.

"Yeah! Me and my girlfriend, Don't worry, my girl friend went to visit her man down New Jersey. She won't be back for a few hours." Sweat trickled down his neck, this time I allowed him to slide his finger into my pussy, just to put him at ease.

"You're sure its safe in there? I mean, I wouldn't want your girl friend to walk in on us." He said all morally. For a second I saw concern in his ayes.

"Nigga, I'm horny! So come on, you see how wet my pussy is. I hope you ain't no two minute brotha," I said, teasing him as we enter the house. Luckily for me the front door was unlocked, and no one was home. We made our way down to the basement.

"Shorty, I'm not playing, no more waiting games. I need to be up in your stomach."

"I want you to know that I'm a real freak, so I hope you're down with what I'm down with, strip!" I wasted no time getting down on my knees, planting a gentle, wet, killer kiss on the crown of his dick. He had his pants down to his ankles in record time. I reached for his pants and took hold of his handcuffs.

"Hold up! Shorty, I'm not into getting tie up or cuffed, up."

"I thought you said you was a freak like me? Beside, when I'm suck your balls and you coming all over my pretty face, I don't want you to try to stop me," I licked my pink lips, while finger fucking myself.

"Handle your business." Captain Brown said, thinking with his little head like most niggas do. He laid back, spreading out his arms. I straddle him and handcuffed both of his hands and feet's.

"Are you ready to find out why they call my Juicy Lips?"

"I been ready!"

"Hold up, let me get some whip cream." I crawled off the bed and want upstairs. I remember seeing a pair of vise-grips. I took them and three hangars. When I came back downstairs, Captain Brown was leaking-*this nigga already busted his nut.*

"You know nigga, you're in for a special treat." I crawled back on the bed, laying the vise-grips on top of his chest, while I untangle the three hangers.

"Bitch! What the fuck are you doing?"

"Chill be, you're about to find out in a second," I replied in my best New York accent. Once I had all three hangers untangle, I wrapped them together around his thick neck.

"Ahhhggghhh," Captain Brown cried out, once he felt the vise grips twisting the hangers tightly, around his neck.

"Scream all the fuck you want. This room is sound proofed. You should know, you been here before. I'm gonna ask you a few questions if you lie, you die, if you tell the truth, I might let you live, its up to you. Where do you work at, and how do you know Estella?" I twisted the vise grip one more time.

"Wait! I'm a correctional officer at Rahway State prison. Estella is just a piece of ass. Her husband introduced me to her."

"Who the fuck is her husband?"

"Some Spanish kid named Diego Laboca!" Captain Brown was willing to tell on God if he had to just to get out of this situation. He stared at me in fear. This shit was like a nightmare to him, as he watched me take the life out of him little by little without being able to do shit about it. *Why did I let this chick cuff me up to the bed? I know I could beat her ass down if I could get my hand loose.*

"Damn shorty, you really gonna let all this dick go to waste?" Captain Brown was using all his seduction techniques. A slight smile crept across his lip.

"In case you haven't figured it out yet, I don't like dicks, I eat pussy. But " I'm gonna make an exception today. I'ma have fun first, then I'm gonna strangle your black ass." He did not answer me. I crawled between his legs and wrapped my lips around the crown of his dick, and wiggle my tongue around his piss hole. Instantly he became rock hard. When I noticed he had his eyes closed enjoying my lips, I backed off, and twisted the vise grips two more knots. His Adam apple was now nervously moving up and down, looking for a release from the tight grip of the hangers.

"Wait! Wait! Wait! Please don't kill me. Please! I got a wife and kids that depend on me." I love to see a grown ass nigga beg for his life. There was some quality to his expression, an ineffable nuance, that told me he was either trying to buy himself some time, or telling me the truth.

"So you lied to me when you said you didn't have a wife. All you men are all the same. You would say anything just to get a piece of pussy. Look at you now! Don't you wish you would've gone home to your wife and kids?!" His tears were real and bitter. They drizzled down his chin, "How does it feel to be powerless? Ain't that how you make the inmates feel, powerless?"

"I-I do my job well"

"So do I," I said with a smile than added, "It against the rules to fuck an inmate wife."

"Diego was a half bitch nigga, a rat, he got what he deserved."

"What do you mean he got what he deserved?"

"Oh, you didn't know, Diego was murdered by another inmate three weeks ago," he said as if I was suppose to feel sorry or something.

"Good! He was worthless rat. By the way, he was my rat and-"

Suddenly I hear the front door open. I looked over at Captain Brown and whispered in' his ear. "If you scream, trust me, I would shoot you in the head. Don't try me!" As a safety precaution I stuffed his own boxers shots in his mouth. I switched the light off and waited.

The foot steps coming down the basement steps were telling that whoever it was wasn't worry about anything. Once the foot steps reached the bottom of the steps, I knew it was a female by the Channel Fragrance. When she reached for the light switch, I went in for the kill, putting her in a choke hold.

"Holy shit! Estella screamed, as she hit the floor.

"Say hello to Justice," I said, pistol whipping her across the right side of her face. The bitch fainted. I cuffed her hands behind her back, and dragged her by the hair to the bed where Captain Brown was laying. I smacked the bitch five times, until she open her eyes with tears leaking from them.

"Who the fuck are you? Estella asked, confused, not fully aware of what was transpiring.

"I'm your worst nightmare. I'm the bitch who decides if you live or die today. So you can consider me God! Estella stomach growl. A spasm of anxiety squeezed at her heart.

"I got a few dollars saved up, you can have them."

"Bitch, this isn't about money! Right now you're about to make the biggest decision of your life. I want you to suck this nigga dick and make him cum within thirty seconds. Failing to do so, will guarantee you a bullet in the back of your head. If you success, both of y'all will get to live another day. Bitch! You better suck that dick like your life depends on it," I said, placing Justice on the back of her head, while she try to deep throat Captain Brown. I smacked her lightly on top of her head, "Bitch, don't cheat. I ain't tell you to start yet. When I say go, you start."

I waited ten seconds before tapping her on the chin with Justice, indicating for her to start.

She began to slide up and down on his dick in a fast motion. Her tongue moved over his shaft, whirled around the tip.

Captain Brown face, was distorted with pleasure. Only if he knew that this would be his last brain job.

"Ten second left, whore!" Estella fluttered her tongue on the upbeat, sucking hard on the down beat.

"Nine! Eight! Seven! Whore, your time is running out." I saw his dick throb against her lips.

"Six second left!" I whispered in her ear.

Oh God, please, I don't want to die! Estella thought as she tighten her lips.

"Five!" *Come on nigga bust your nut. This ain't the time to prolong it.* Estella sucking pace picked up, saliva was dripping from the corner of her mouth.

"Four! Three! Two!" Estella moved her head back, and her mouth was full of cum. It trickle from the corner of her mouth. I looked at her and winked. She smiled as if she had accomplished her life, long dream.

"You got a good head game, go on and finish him off." Once she had him back down her throat, I pulled the trigger on Justice, cracking her melon in half. Captain Brown passed out when he felt her brains all over him. I gripped Justice tightly and started knocking his teeth out of his mouth. He moaned, which indicated to me that he was still alive. I ran back upstairs and grabbed a pair of shears. I leaned over the bed and grabbed what was left of Estella head and throw her down on the floor, and began hacking away at Captain Brown dick. The shears were nice and sharp, so his dick fell off on the first try. I then twisted the vise grips until his eyes were yellow and red, ready to pop out of the sockets. His tongue hanged out of his mouth. I picked up his dick from the bed and stuffed in his mouth. *Karma is a muthafucka*, I said, as I walked out the basement and out of Diego house with my pussy hole dripping. The fabric of my tong rubbed against my swollen clit, sending erotic chill along my spine. *I might have to see a psychiatric, cause every time I offed one of these worthless, bastards, I get wet and horny.*

CHAPTER 18
"Urban Jungle"

District Attorney Office…

"Whoever is trying to set me up, without a doubt is trying to end my political career. I knew Peter Newman is behind all this. But who's doing his dirty work?" Charles Krinsky asked the newly elective District Attorney in Philadelphia, Francis Williams.

"Charles, tell me something I don't know! You white boys up in Harrisburg are always getting yourself in some political scandals, then you're run to the black man for help," Francis said, adjusting his reading glasses.

Two years older than Charles Krinsky, Francis Williams had come up in the streets of West Philadelphia. He came up under the wings of the original black Mafia, better known, as Brother's Incorporated. He dodged bullets, ran coke packages, gone hungry, and seen the down side of the street game first hand. With the money he earned from his street hustles, he put himself through Temple Law School, graduating summa cum laude. After two years in the District Attorneys offices, as assistance D.A., he became a rising star with a conviction rate that was untouchable.

"Francis," said Charles, who coughed and then blew his nose, "this is serious. Right now I'm ahead on all the polls. I can't afford no fuck up's! If I win, you will win, also. My people has ensure me, that on Tuesday November second, you will make history again, as the first "Black African American elective District Attorney in Philadelphia, for two terms.

Cracker! I'm going to be elective either way. Blacks and Hispanics are fed up with Lee Abraham bullshit! Mumia supporters are angry, because this Jew bitch does nothing but look out for the white boys in the city. Her time is up! Y'all crackers are about to paid restitution to all blacks and Hispanics in the city when I get in office, Francis thought to himself as he rustled through some papers while Charles Krinsky stared at him in silence.

"Charles, one hand washes the other. I have been holding you down since our college's days. When you came to work in this office, I showed you how to get blacks and Hispanics defendants to plead bargain, just so that you could build your record. Big black Williams always protect you. So when your ass get to the governors mansion, I'ma need you to assign my wife to a cabinet position. Maybe assign her to be secretary of correction. I'm sure all the brothers who you falsely put in prison would appreciate it."

Charles Krinsky looked up at me in surprise. "But I must be careful, I-"

"Charles, you are going to be the fucking governor! The boss of the state!" Francis hunched forward, "I been hearing the rumors amongst our associates, and trust me, you're not well licked. But I like you."

Charles shook his head as if he was offended.

"What rumors?"

"Charles, you always been a bad boy. I don't give a damn about your personal life style. I'm your friend," Francis said with a smile.

Charles started feeling a little better when he heard the word friend. He assumed that Francis will assist him. He needed to know who Peter Newman had doing his dirty work. It was known within the law community that Peter Newman had some undercover sniper lady, agent, cleaning shit up in Philly.

'Who's this damn bitch?" Francis asked, showing concern, putting on a strong front.

"I don't know who she is. Don't nobody in our cycle of associates know her identity." Charles Krinsky said.

"Don't worry about it buddy, I would have my snitches in the streets look into this. If this sniper, lady agent, is in this city, somebody got to know who she is."

Charles Krinsky sat back and smiled. "So I guess there's nothing else to discuss." He got up and left the District Attorney office feeling excited.

**The Doughnut Shop on 52nd Street,
Near Market Street...**

Charles sat at the far end of the doughnut shop. All, eyes were on him. He was there to enjoy a cup of coffee and a few jelly doughnuts. A few of the customers walked past his table and made smart remarks.

"Yeah! There goes that asshole!" One black lady in her 70's said to the waitress as she headed out the door.

"I told you not to support that punk fagot! He should be ashamed of himself," another customer yelled.

The best thing about America is that people have the right to express their dislike towards any political candidates. Charles Krinsky thought to himself as he open a copy of the Philadelphia Inquire Newspaper and began reading it from the back. He went straight to the sport section. Michael Vick and the Philadelphia Eagles, historic win over the New York Giants was the cover story. Finally, after forty minutes of reading every section of the paper, he made his way to the front section, page one.

His appetite for coffee and jelly doughnuts quickly disappeared. His eyes widen, his mouth almost drop to the floor. He reread the headlines, two times! Three times! four times! Five times, before he decided to read the entire article, and closely study the three photos. He lifted his head off the paper and looked around the doughnut shop, and clearly understood why everyone was staring at him. *How could this be happening to me? How could this be possible?*

He pulled out his cell phone from the inside of his jacket and pressed his speed dial. Peter Newman pick up his phone on the first ring.

"Peter, did you seen the article? Did you seen the paper today?"

"Congratulation, buddy, you're the breaking news story. Every paper in the city has your face on it. Every news station is giving you free publicity. You even made national news. CNN is running a special on you. Asshole! Didn't I told you to stay clean until after the election?"

"But-But-those photos are fake. What the article is saying is a lie."

"Who care if it's true or not. In politic, perception is everything. If we lose these elections because of your stupid, careless, freak behavior, I will personally kick your ass. You're famous now, asshole!" Peter Newman said with a smile. He wanted to laugh out loud, but he didn't want Charles Krinsky to feel as if he was clowning him. "This isn't fair!" "Hey! Nobody said life was fair."

"Can we make this go away?" Charles asked. His mind weary with questions without answers.

"Do you want my suggestion?" Peter asked. His voice escaping from him like helium from a balloon.

"Yeah!"

"Don't be ridiculous," Peter Newman said, before he could stop himself. He looked over at me and rolled up the Philadelphia Inquire News paper, and threw it in the waste basket, and added, "If I was you, I lawyer up. How does it feel now?" He sat back in his stylish comfortable, leather chair and threw his feet's upon the highly polished mahogany burl deco table. "To be a star."

Charles closed his eyes, not believing what he was hearing on the other side of the phone. Although he was a media whore, the last thing he wanted was to be trust into the media spotlight a month before election on a child pornography accusation. He was struggling to maintain his composure. He tried to think, but his mind was cluttered with images of the three photos, showing him rubbing the private's parts of three little girls who were all under the age of five.

I watched Peter Newman, fascinated with how he was breaking Charles Krinsky down, mentally.

"Peter, I know one of your people put this bullshit out there, I thought-"

"White boy! You may be the top dog up in Harrisburg, but you mean absolutely nothing to me. I been watching you for some time now! All I was waiting for, was for you to fuck up. I'm tired of cleaning up after you. Slavery is over, white boy! But I kinda like you."

"In other words, you want this mess to disappear?" Charles asked.

"I want it cleaned it up. Do it anyway you want. I don't want the media to air any more of your dirty laundry. Do you understand me?"

"Yeah!"

Get your people to do some damage control, you'll be alright. I'm sure Pennsylvanians will forgive you for your shortcomings," Peter Newman said, closing his phone shut, not giving Charles the opportunity to keep running his mouth. He then turned towards me and said, "November 2nd. 2010 will forever be remember. I truly believe this pending scandal will rock the entire political infrastructure of Pennsylvania."

"I'm looking forward to it. I got enough, hard evidence against him, that even if he hire Kelvin Mosantos the best attorney in this state! Or even if he bring Johnny Cochran back from the grave, the bastard don't stand a chance. By the way, did you like the photos? They are a little disturbing, and fascinated all at once. They bring out all the worst instinct in a person. I be surprise if he wins the election on November 2nd."

"Take it from me, I know how them white people in rural areas in Pennsylvania think. They rather vote a white pervert into office, than to vote for a city guy. By six o'clock, Charles political team will put a different spin on things." Peter said, his breath coming in hard, little bursts.

"Will see on November 2nd!"

"I can't wait! I can't wait!" Peter tried to laugh, but the sound got caught in his throat.

"Get out of my business establishment you're a pervert," a high yellow negro with freckles on his face, said as he approached the table Charles was sitting at. Charles glanced up at the man and nodded his head.

"How much for the coffee and doughnuts?"

"Cracker! Didn't you hear me say get out of my business establishment!"

With a curse, "Son of a bitch!" Charles got up from the chair and slowly walked towards the door, walking out the doughnut shop, into the urban jungle where an uncertainty reality awaited him. His whole brain fell into a chaotic jumble; for the first time in his life he felt all his hidden fears rushing in on him. His eyes became watery and gleaming, as he remembered a saying his deceased father use to tell him, "Never let other man impose their will on you. If you allow it, your life is not worth living." Charles sat in his car for five hours, thinking about his next move. He sensed that the end of his political career was finally coming. *Stop being a soft mothafucking coward! Man the fuck up! Face your enemies!* His conscious was stroking his ago, and talking mad shit to him.

Back In My Apartment...

As I sat in silence in Jasmine apartment, I was seriously thinking of going through the whole house and see what I could find. I knew this bitch was sitting on some paper, she had to! Who in this fucking world give away eighteen thousand dollars? Why did she leave the four packages of pills out in the open? She wants to test me. Something is out of cynic! This whole apartment look like it can be use for an advertisement in a magazine. Fuck it, I 'ma play this one safe. I 'ma show this bitch that I could be trusted. I laid my head back on the couch and instantly began to dream. I could see my mothers face as clearly as if she was sitting beside me. I could hear her voice "Bitch get the fuck outa my house." I awoke surprised and gratified, that I been able to sleep without having to fight off my adopted father, who on most nights wanted me to suck him off. I extended my hand, and was about to get up from the couch, when I noticed Jasmine staring at me from the corner of the living room.

"How long have you been watching me?"

"I been here for about two hours, now. I didn't want to wake you up. You shoulda lay down on my bed."

I was feeling good, horny, and ready to release some stress. After noticing Yanira, I never made it past the living room, I got the feeling that she wasn't as dumb as she appeared to be. I got to keep my guard up with this little bitch! She may look like a child, but her mind is razor sharp, fueled by a deep desire to hustle hard and do what she had to do to survive. I made a mental note to keep Yanira on a tight leash.

"You never told me to lay down on your bed, so I waited for you here!" Yanira replied with a serious look, giving me the *bitch-you-think-I-was-gonna-rob-your-place-look*.

"Ah, you're such a sweet girl."

"Listen, I don't want you to feel pity for me. I refuse to accept any hand outs. I like to earn everything I get in life. Don't let my pretty face fool you, I can get down and dirty." Yanira said. Her words had the hairs on the back of my neck standing.

I had dealt with a lot of homicidal maniacs in my line of work to be fool by a cute face. The look in her eyes told me she wasn't bluffing about getting dirty.

"How dirty have you gotten?"

"A girl should never share her secretes. But put it this way, I don't believe In God-Jesus, whatever you call it, because after all, in my book, God was a man, and in this world, man cannot be trusted. Therefore, I have no problems taking care of myself," a slight smile crept across her lips.

This young rider has no clue that I'm about to test her

gangster. Philadelphia is such a fuck up city that one never knows where the next wave of violence is coming from. Philly is also a breeding ground for some of the most vicious killers. The latest, twenty two years old Antonio Rodriguez, better known to the people in North Philly, as the Kensington Strangler, who specialized, in raping and strangling white prostitutes. But, if I have it my way, Yanira will become my shadow, my mini me, a cold-blooded predator who will kill for the sheer joy of it.

"You're clever!"

"Why you said that?"

"Because you didn't answer my question."

"Read between the lines."

"I did!"

"And?"

"To be honest with you, I'm still not convinced you could get dirty and grimy, you're too pretty!"

Yanira rummage around in her bag. She pulled out a small wallet. Before she could open it, a photograph fell to the floor of a wig, wearing Puerto Rican lady, who appeared to have too much make up on her face. Yanira did not want to look at the photo, but she didn't have a choice, whether she believed in God or not, her power and conviction were about to be tested, sooner than she thought. Yanira felt the rage rising within her, until she was in a blind fury.

"If I was to bump heads with this nasty, looking

whore, I swear to God I will beat her to death with my bare hands."

"Who is she?"

"It don't even matter! It's because of her I been through so much bullshit in life. One day I'm going to make her life miserable."

"Is she your mother?" I asked, but I already knew the answer.

"Yeah!" Yanira said, handing me the photo. The second I looked at it my eyes flinched. What a small world. The whore in the photo was the same whore in the hotel lobby where Ted Connors was murdered. The whore was none other than Charles Krinsky, wife's cousin, mistress, Philadelphia police Department top whore.

"Baby girl, your enemies are my enemies. I swear to you that I will help you out." Just by looking at Yanira, I knew she needed a little reassurance. I handed her back the photo. When she went to put it back into her wallet, another photo fell out. This time, my mouth hung wide open. The photo was identical to the one I used to frame Charles Krinsky.

"Oh, that's me when I was about five years old!"

"It's beautiful."

"I always been a cute girl. That photo was use on a Sear's commercial. I always wanted to be a star," Yanira said flirtatiously. That explain why it was on the internet. I just hope it don't come back to bits me on the ass.

Don't worry about it baby girl! You're already famous,
you just don't know it yet. In a few days your photo will be the
solid reason for bringing down the Governor of Pennsylvania,
the most racist state in the union.

"Baby girl, you are already a star! Tomorrow you will
turn eighteen, which make you legal for a lot of things," I
said, seductively, "I'ma go ahead and take me a rest. If you
want you can laid on my bed with me-"

"I'ma watch BET for a little while. I'll be here when
you wake up from your rest."

Twelve-O-One Midnight, October 25, 2010...

I awoke to the sound of the shower running. I took
my panties off and tip-toed to the bathroom. Yanira stood
under the water as it splashed against her body. My tongue
became extra wet as I thought about what I was about to
do. She never noticed me step into the bathroom, until I
was in the shower with her. I was brutal, "Bent over so I
could get a taste of your pussy!" I could see that she was
too frozen by the situation, so I took charge. I moved my
hands over her knees, parting her legs wide open. Then
I slid my tongue between the lips of her young pussy,
giving her a jolt of electricity as I wiggled it. I sucked her
clit between my lips and bit on it lightly. Then I lifted her
round ass cheeks in the palms of my hand and moved
by head low, letting my tongue slide on the button of her

asshole with short round motion of my tongue. Yanira had an orgasm almost instantly.

"Ooooooo, I can't believe how beautifully you do that." Yanira almost fainted from the intensity. Her body responded to my tongue perfectly. She was turned the fuck out, and there was no turning back.

CHAPTER 19

"Someone Please Call 911"

Mari De Lasantos navigated her wheelchair up the ramp of the women's shelter down 10th and Erie Avenue, and unlocked the door to her first floor apartment.

For the last year, she had been battling spine cancer which left her confined to a wheelchair, and with a number of health issues and kidney and liver ailments. Mari had outlived the predictions of her doctors. She knew that her time was coming. Her organs were giving up on her the same way she'd been giving up on her daughter.

Despite her confinement to a wheelchair, the whore still had the meanest head game in Philly. She had sucked so many dicks in North Philly that she had gained a new nickname, "Cripple Mouth".

After hours of watching TV and waiting on her friend, Lusty, Mari started nodding off. The damn medication was finally taking a toll. She thought she heard the door open and figured that it was Lusty or one of the other overpaid counselors at the shelter coming to change her diaper. These young bitches who worked as counselors didn't give a fuck about the people they were supposed to care for, even though they made outrageous tax payer money. Not to mention the shit they steal from the patients on a daily basis.

Damn! Her back was killing her. She tried to navigate her wheelchair towards her tiny bedroom to pick up her ringing cell phone, but her vision was so blurred and her body began doing funny things. She finally got scared when she turned her wheelchair around to head back to the living room and bumped into the wall. Her wheelchair flipped over. She was sure that she heard the door and footsteps. "Help! Help!" she called out. "Lusty, is that you?" She thought she heard approaching footsteps, but no one ever came.

Suddenly, she heard the words, "I believe we have unfinished business."

Mari was sprawled across the floor, breathing heavily. She tried to focus her eyes on the subject in front of her. She even tried to utter the words, "Who the fuck are you?" but, couldn't find her breath.

I inserted an asthma pump that sat on the table in the living room into her mouth. I needed her to be aware and to feel what I had in store for her. I was so enraged just by looking at her that I began kicking her in the left eye. Every kick I delivered to her face represented the many times I had to fuck and suck to survive. I kept kicking her face to the floor until her nose was a flatten pulp of cartilage.

"Come on, Mom. Get the fuck up! I'm giving you a fighting chance! I'm gonna give you the chance you never gave me. Oh, my bad! Now your ass is crippled, so you can't get up, huh?" I put my finger on her wrist and the whore was still alive. I whispered in her ear, "I want my face to be the last thing you see before you die!" I thought I saw her lips move, so I kept stomping her face until I saw chunks of her brain on the bottom of Jasmine Prada boots, and blood pouring out of her ears.

"Is that all you got?" Jasmine asked me, glaring at me with a look on her face that I wasn't accustomed to seeing. At that point, I got the feeling that she was a little jealous that she was not partaking in the demise of my mother. Jasmine couldn't quite see it, and if she did, she didn't acknowledge that her brilliant career of being a grimy bitch was dying off, while mine had begun to blossom. I looked at her and smiled.

I dragged my mother's motionless, crippled body by her hair into the bathroom and placed what was left of her face in the shit bowl. I then turned the portable radio on that sat on a shelf in the bathroom to Q-102 and ironically, Wyclef Jean's classic song was playing:

"...If this is the life my momma warned me about,
I'm in trouble. I'm in real trouble.
Someone please call 911..."

I betrayed no hint of the emotional stress I'd been feeling since my mother threw my ass out on the streets, butt as naked. At that single moment, I realized that I was no longer a child.

I took one last glance at my mother, and immediately realized that my past was gone, and there was nothing anyone could say or do to change it. I now had to look towards the future. And the question in my mind was, *What would that future be?*

Half Hour later:..

"Yanira, I know you probably don't want to talk about it right now, but I want to congratulate you for the ass kicking you dished out to your mother," I said as I reached into my bag and pulled out my .50-caliber Desert Eagle handgun and handed it to her, then added, "You see, baby girl, what you did today is what most girls dream of doing. You're cut out for this line of work. The government will train you and pay you well for this kind of work." I then handed her my CIA credentials.

"Oh shit! You're the goddamn pop-pop, huh?" I

didn't say a word. Yanira just inclined her head faintly to indicate that she couldn't believe what she was seeing.

I smiled, because behind her pretty face, a nondescript, vicious beast waited to be released. In this cruel world, you're either the victim, or the victimizer. This young chick definitely had the heart to be a ruthless bitch.

I surveyed the street, giving Yanira enough time to absorb the heavy load I just dropped in her lap. Finally, after an awkward silence, I spoke. "No! I'm not the police. I'm a CIA Agent for the United Sneak of America. I've got a code of honor I live by: Whatever I do, I do for a reason."

"Gotcha! But why didn't you tell me from the rip? You gave me the impression that you were an around the way chick, and—"

"I am an around the way chick. That's what makes my job so easy to do."

"It doesn't make any sense. I mean, you gave me drugs to sell, and—"

"Baby girl, life makes no sense sometimes. What matters is that we both share a secret that I would take to the grave with me. You could either ride with me and get rich in the process, or you could get the fuck out of my car and keep it moving," I said, looking Yanira dead in her eyes. They said that the eyes are the windows of your soul. If this is true, then Yanira's were exposing her innermost thoughts, because I read right through her. *I hope this young, still wet behind the ears chick don't make me put one in her spinal cord. Her decision will determine if she lives or dies today. If she stays, she lives. If she acts funny, I'm just gonna cap her wig back.*

"I guess I'm tainted goods, but I'm all for allowing the grass to grow under my feet. Grass always gets greener later on."

"Nah, baby girl, you're not tainted goods," I said, trying to hold back the leaking between my legs. I was brought to reality when I heard a tap on the glass. Not giving it too much attention, I rolled the window down, and instantly I felt cold metal against my temple.

""Yeah, bitch! I caught you slipping! Talk dat tough Tony shit to me now!" William said as he pimp slapped me in the mouth.

"Damn! This nigga is really feeling himself. Sweet Lips musta done this asshole dirty for real! "Yo, I told you before, I don't even know who the fuck you are! You're mistaking me for somebody else, so chill with that shit!" I said, trying to push the gun away from my head. *If this nigga even blinks for a second, I'ma body him!*

"Oh, you still want to play dumb and act like you don't know me, huh? Both of you bitches get out the car now, 'fore I start busting y'all asses!"

"What if we don't wanna get out of the car?" Yanira asked, giving William the middle finger.

"Then, you'll be the first bitch to die!" William said.

Yanira and I both opened the car doors at the same time. William kept his hand wrapped around my throat and his gun pressed against my temple.

"Nigga, you sure you want to go this far?"

"Bitch, I'm gonna make you remember me." He backed up a few steps and ordered me to drop my pants. I just stared at him. "You could either drop your pants, or take one in the back of your head. Come on, bitch! Drop your pants!" William pulled his dick out.

No words needed to be spoken to know what he had planned. He wanted to humiliate me. I dropped my pants to my ankles and stood by my car.

"Bitch, where is my baby?"

"Your baby is dead, nigga!"

William's face turned red, his eyes widened, and for a split second, he focused all his attention towards me. He never saw it coming when Yanira fired a bullet from the .50-caliber Desert Eagle handgun I had given her in the car, in the back of his head. She got closer and grabbed him by the hair as he fell, then fired two more bullets into his throat. At that moment, I no longer saw a tainted, confused young lady. I was witnessing the making of a cold heartless bitch.

"Are you alright?" I asked Yanira.

"I'm good. That clown back there musta been on a death wish. Well, he got what he was looking for. That was just an example of how dirty I could get."

"I don't have any sympathy for him either," I replied, giving Yanira wink as a sign of approval. She had officially been damaged forever.

CHAPTER 20

"Judgment Day"

Election Day, November 2, 2010...

Six o'clock in the morning, Charles Krinsky knew that this would be the best day of his life. He wanted to be the first one in the voting booth. All weekend long he had been ducking reporters who were trying to question him about the photos, which the media had dubbed, "Innocence Lost".

Reporters had been lurking around his house, waiting for him. They wanted to give the voters the cruel reality of their elected officials.

As soon as he opened the door to his house, Charles bumped into a sea of people. Fox 29 News had set up a camera crew to broadcast the entire spectacle live.

"Sir! Mr. Governor to be!" said the reporter. "Look, I know this is probably a really awkward time, but your supporters want to know about the recent photos published in the *Philadelphia Inquirer*."

Charles didn't answer.

"Come on! You're a coward!" said the reporter. "We deserve answers!"

Charles turned around and said, "I will give a full press conference tonight. Right now, all I want to do is get to the voting booth."

"Sir, I'm giving you a shot to tell your side of the story here. Fair and square. According to our inside sources, one of the victims in the photos — now an adult — will be giving an exclusive interview to CNN tonight."

Charles stopped in his tracks when he heard the words, "One of the victims" slide off the reporter's lips. "Don't journalism rules call for some measurement of fairness? Those photos are phony, and whatever victim comes forward could only be a fabricated one. I'm being framed!"

"Well, sir, we the people have every reason to believe that you are a child predator with no business running for public office, let alone governor. You don't deserve the courtesy of the medial. Unlike you, we reporters have rules which are called professional ethics."

"Rot in hell!" a black lady shouted in a voice loud enough to make the crowd around stop what they were doing and stare. The black lady in front of the reporter spit in his face.

Charles didn't even bother to wipe away the spit. The camera crew and other reporters were screaming for him to look their way so they could take his picture. Some even blocked his path to his car.

"Get the fuck out of my way!" Charles yelled.

"Did you get that? Did you get that?" another reporter yelled.

"Are you assholes gonna help or not?" Charles yelled at the three undercover police officers who were assigned to protect him. He pushed through the crowd and hopped into his BMW, started it up, rolled the window down and yelled at the reporters, "Y'all all invited to attend the party tonight after I'm elected the 46th Governor of this state!"

A slew of cell phones started snapping pictures and recording what was about to become a You Tube sensation.

That Same night, 8:30 P.M...

"Breaking news. Fox 29 has just learned that many of the polls are showing that Republican candidate for governor, Charles Kirnsky, is leading in every poll across the state. Reliable sources are saying that Krinsky will be our next governor. When the polls close at ten, Fox 29 will bring you full coverage."

"Inside sources are also confirming that the Justice Department is keeping a close eye on this

race, because Mr. Krinsky has a dark cloud over him
due to recent photos that show him inappropriately
touching three five-year-old girls. The FBI has
already confirmed that the photos are authentic."
   "This is Dave Schratweiser for Fox 29 News."

The next piece of news footage showed Charles Krinsky cursing and pushing a reporter. The speed of the footage made him look almost as if he was smiling. The most cinematographic moment was when he rolled his car window down and invited reporters to the party. Each word that fell off his lips appeared to be in slow motion.

I sat in Peter Newman's office, listening to him go over last minute preparations with the Philadelphia District Attorney, Francis Williams. My pussy hole was on fire. I stared daggers at Peter Newman for having me in his office.

Francis Williams was such an egotistical asshole that he didn't even acknowledge my presence. To him, a female was a benefit to him. I certainly would have been reluctant to talk if asked to for fear that my identity might become publicly known. It would be in no one's best interest for such a thing to happen. From experience, I know that no politician in Philadelphia can be trusted, and Francis Williams was no different. The nigga was corrupt to the core.

   "Francis, I want you to know and understand how

much there is at stake here. I will make sure your office gets full credit, and the first shot at prosecuting Charles for child pornography, but the Feds get first dibs at the murder charge. I will also make sure that your wife gets assigned to the position of Secretary of Corrections. That way, you can help your people," Peter Newman said, raising his fist high in the air.

Show Time, 9:00 P.M...

A cluster of news camera crews and field correspondents had parked in front of Charles Krinsky's headquarters down in Center City, Philadelphia, where he was supposed to make an acceptance speech and thank all of his supporters. The crowd of mainly old, rich white people with a sense of entitlement celebrated, by hugging and kissing each other.

Thirty minutes later, the crowd erupted in applause when Charles Krinsky appeared on sage with a rented wife, and some rented kids. The room went silent.

"Sometimes in life, you will face adversity, and that's when you must stand fast on your belief in God and trust that He will guide you through. In the last week, people have painted me to be a monster, but—"

Peter Newman and I quietly made our way to the front of the stage. Undercover FBI Agents had the front of the stage surrounded, ready for the takedown.

Charles Krinsky went on. "I'm ready to face adversity! The voters have spoken, and today I stand before you as your new elected Governor, and I—"

Charles Krinsky's eyes widened when he saw me standing beside him on the stage. I shook my head, letting him know that the party was about to be over. He ignored me and kept speaking. "Would never compromise my principles or take shortcuts. I'm prepared to make Pennsylvania a better place for all of us, and—"

My eyes were hard and cold. I just about heard enough. I grabbed the microphone out of his hand and addressed his constituents, who were looking at me as if I was crazy. "Ladies and gentlemen, this party is over!" I then turned around to face Charles, looked him straight in the eyes and said, "Mr. Governor, congratulations. You are under arrest for the murder of CIA Director Ted Connors. You have the right to remain silent—"

"I'm the damn governor! You can't arrest me!"

"Anything you say can and will be used against you in a court of law. If—"

"I'm being framed! I'm innocent!"

"You can't afford a lawyer; the state will provide one for you. Do you—"

"Fuck you! You stupid spic bitch! I will have your job by tomorrow morning! You can't arrest me!"

"Understand your—"

"This is injustice!"

"Rights?"

"This spic bitch is framing me! I have rights! Goddamn it, I have rights!"

I leaned forward as I was cuffing him and whispered in his ear, "You're the sorriest human being I've ever seen. I hope those niggas in prison bend your ass over and tear your ass out of the farm, then shank you up 'til they blow out your candles, you son of a bitch!"

"Get your hands off of me! I have rights!"

"Mr. Governor, I guess it's true what they say, that everyone loses some times."

"Never me, bitch! I have rights!" he shouted all they way out of his headquarters and into the unmarked car waiting for him. His pale white skin had turned bright red with anger.

Being the grimy bitch that I pride myself to be, I don't ever go into a mission with the idea of defeating the person I'm after. I specialize in defeating a person's confidence. A person with doubts can not focus on victory. Two muthafuckas are considered equal only when they both have equal confidence.

As y'all could see, most of the bitch ass men I take down do not have the confidence it takes to fuck with a grimy bitch like me. Make no mistake about it. I'm still Queen Bee! The coldest bitch ever in Philadelphia!

Turn the page for an exciting

Sneak Peek Of

DAMAGED 3
"The Making Of A Heartless Bitch"

CHAPTER 1

"The Pig Is On Fire"

I was transported down to the FBI headquarters on Market Street in downtown Philadelphia. I was rushed in through a side door.

"You're getting booked tonight at the Federal courthouse," the spic bitch who cuffed me up said.

"I want to see my lawyer! I believe that I have the right to make a phone call."

"Mr. Governor, are you crazy, or are you fucking stupid? You don't have any fucking rights. You don't get shit! The only thing you are entitled to is an asshole full of time. I got bad news for you. Not even Johnny Cochran— if he comes back from the grave—would be able to save your white, cracker ass! In case you don't know, Mr. Governor, I don't exist. You don't even know my name. Once I leave here, you will never see me again. If I want to, I could pay your rented wife and kids a visit and make them disappear from the face of the Earth."

"You spic bitch! You will rot in hell!"

"I believe you will get to hell before me."

Two FBI Agents showed up to the holding cell and asked me if the prisoner was ready. I smiled. "Mr. governor, you are about to get a taste of what them niggas and Puerto Ricans go through every day in the criminal justice system. Kangaroo Court!" I said kicking him in the nuts and sending him straight to the floor, face first. I walked out of the cell feeling horny as hell. I couldn't wait to get home to my new young piece of ass.

Twenty Minutes Later:..

I sat in the back of an empty court while our 46th governor stood in an orange jumpsuit, looking like a fucking clown in front of a black judge, who appeared to be more than happy to be given the opportunity to pull a Willie Lynch move on a political big wig, who was known in the City of Philadelphia as the "Black Man's Nightmare". When Charles Krinsky was the DA in Philly, he prosecuted more blacks and Hispanics than any other prosecutors.

"Mr. Krinsky, you are being arraigned for three counts of endangering the welfare of a child, and murder in the first degree. Due to the nature of the crimes, bail is denied. So, how do you plead?" the judge asked, staring Charles Krinsky in the eyes.

"Your Honor, my lawyer isn't even here! This whole process is a violation of my Constitutional rights! I want to speak to my attorney, now!" Charles Krinsky's legs wobbled. He wanted to scream, but once he saw the two FBI Agents standing by his side ready to restrain him, he calmed his ass down fast. The only words that seemed to slid out of his mouth were, "I'm not guilty!"

"Mr. Krinsky, do you understand that you can face the death penalty?"

"Your Honor, you're outta your mind!" he soberly responded.

"I may be out of my mind, but tonight, you won't be celebrating. The only place you will be going is to the Federal Detention Center. Have a safe trip to your new house!"

"But, Your Honor, I'm not guilty!"

"That's what they all say. Save all the drama for trial."

Federal Detention Center:...

Being as though this was a high profile case, I was isolated from the rest of the population. The only prisoners allowed to roll around in the unit where I was housed were the runners, snitches and rats, who were also isolated because they were witnesses for the government in other high profile cases.

Twenty three and one was the norm. Every meal was brought to my cell. Showers were every other day.

As the only white person on the unit, I was constantly being threatened by black and Hispanic inmates. Names such as "baby rapist", "honky", "cracker", "white faggot" or "top cop" were yelled towards my cell at all hours of the day. There were plenty of times when I thought about hanging the fuck up with my bed sheets. Even the highly trained federal officers got their shit off by spitting in my food tray or pissing in my coffee cup. Three weeks since my arrival, and it felt like three decades.

"Mr. Governor, are you taking a shower today?" the new Hispanic officer asked me.

I looked at her through my cell door and immediately felt that something was wrong. *I never saw this guard before. Plus, normally all prisoners are handcuffed and shackled up before they are let out of their cells. So, why is she just opening my cell?* I thought to myself as I stepped out of my cell in my boxer shorts and my federal issue towel around my neck.

"Sir, these monsters are 'bout to rain down on your ass!" I heard the Hispanic guard say as she left me out on the tier by myself.

I saw a big black nigga — a Muslim — coming my way, and instantly my bowels gave up on me. Shit was running down the crack of my ass, and hot urine trickled down my legs.

"Mr. Governor, can you pardon my life sentence? Can you get me out of here, cracker?" he asked.

Then, the big Muslim nigga flipped the cap on a plastic Suave Shampoo bottle, and sprayed the contents all over my body, from head to toe. I smelled the gasoline. I tried to push him away, but he beat the shit out of me. I saw the hate in his eyes. The lighter did what it was supposed to do. I felt my body melting. I could barely move. I was choking on the smoke from my own burning skin.

The smell of bacon penetrated the tier. Cellblock E erupted. The rest of the prisoners began banging on their cell doors.

"Allaah-U-Akbar! Allaah-U-Akbar!" one FOI (Fruit of Islam) yelled.

"Die, cracker! Another joined.

"You fucking pig! Die!" the Black Muslim who lit my ass on fire said before he struck me on the neck with a sharp object.

"Help! Fire!" I yelled to no avail.

"The pig! The pig! The pig is on fire! We don't need no water. Let the fucking rapist burn! Burn, rapist, burn! Burn!" the cellblock chanted.

NEW VISION
PUBLICATION
PRESENTS
NEW YORK
A
BLIND
Shot
A NOVEL BY
JANEI

Chapter One

The car moved slowly through the streets of Harlem, in New York City. Its two occupants were watching as merchants closed their stores for the night. The sun had set an hour ago, but the sidewalk remained crowded with people. They surveyed block after block like tourists fascinated by the sights and sounds of an urban legend. Trey and Butter were far from that. Nor were they new-comers in this part of town. Both of them were born in Harlem Hospital and raised in the surrounding neighborhoods, from Central Park North up into the Polo Grounds. They knew their way around these streets like the backs of their hands.

A few girls standing around glanced at their ten year old Mazda and quickly dismissed the both of them as nobodies. In truth, these two had quite a reputation, though an anonymous one. They were the stick-up men that had robbed at least a dozen grocery stores, drug spots, and jewelry-wearing cash-heavy ballers in the last month alone.

Trey had the radio blasting hardcore gangsta rap,

as he played with the barrel of a Magnum he held out of sight of onlookers. Butter maneuvered the Mazda down several side streets and came to a stop at a red light. On the corner, several young Black men were laughing and joking at a card table. A small radio near them atop a milk crate was playing oldies. The loud music from the Mazda caught their attention as it idled at the light. Trey stared hard at them, and eventually he was noticed and the men stared back.

Finally, one of them yelled to him, "What the fuck you looking at, man?"

As the light changed, Trey pointed the Magnum at the men, and they all dove to the ground for cover. With one shot, he blasted their tiny radio to bits. The roar of the Magnum echoed on the street. As the men continued to hug the ground, Trey could be heard laughing over the sound of the car's music as the Mazda sped away.

Trey, at twenty-two years old, had spent half of his life in and out of jail. He was never without a gun. He got his first taste of its power when he got his hands on the .357 Magnum while in junior high school. One day, he watched as a local heroin dealer named Dax ran from cops, and tossed the gun under an old dirty mattress. After the police caught Dax five blocks away, beat him and hauled him off to jail, Trey retrieved the weapon. The first thing he noticed was how heavy it was, but it was beautiful and he instantly fell in love with it. He carried it all the time, even to school, and waited for the opportunity to use it.

One day, there were some school bullies picking on some weaker kids. Then, they approached Trey. They told him he was going to have to start paying punk dues if he wanted to continue to come to school. Though Trey was never fond of school in the first place, he saw this as what he had been waiting for. He pulled out the Magnum, and before any of them could react, he smashed the biggest one across the face with the heavy weapon. As the kid lay on the ground holding his shattered jaw, Trey stripped him and his friends of money, jewelry and every stitch of clothing, then sent them running home bare ass naked.

He was arrested the next day, and although they never got the Magnum, he was charged and convicted of assault and robbery. At thirteen, he began his journey in and out of juvenile detention and prison.

Butter, on the other hand, fared well growing up. Though older than Trey at twenty-seven, he had never been arrested, even though he had been pulling robberies for years. Butter was always a thinker and a planner, and was often willing to pull a job if it could be done with the least amount of violence.

He had met Trey two years ago when he worked for a job center in the Harlem State Office Building. Trey was on parole at the time and was required to get a job. He began visiting the center just to keep his parole officer off his back. Butter, who did filing and record keeping, talked to Trey every time he came by, and the two started hanging out. Before long, Butter began to join Trey on the armed robberies he boasted so much about.

Butter grew to not only appreciate the money they made, but the thrill and cunningness of robbing so many people and never getting caught. It became a game to him. Yet, Trey's explosive and sometimes violent temper spoiled that fun, and more than once he put them both at risk of getting killed.

Now, as they cruised down the streets of Harlem to the next job, he willed everything to go as planned.

After several more turns, Butter finally parked the car across the street from an old tenement. He reached over and turned off the radio...

NEW VISION
PUBLICATION

P.O. Box 2815
Stockbridge, GA 30281

Or

P.O. Box 310367
Jamaica, NY 11431

Order Form

Name: _____

Address: _____

City: _____ **State:** _____ **Zip:** _____

Qty	Title	Price	Total
	Tit 4 Tat	$15.00	
	A Blind Shot	$15.00	
	Damaged	$15.00	
	Tit 4 Tat 2	$15.00	
	Boss Lady	$15.00	
	Shank	$15.00	
	Unfaithful To The Game	$15.00	
	Tit 4 Tat 3	$15.00	
	Still Damaged	$15.00	
	- Coming Soon -		
	Thicker Than Blood	$15.00	
	...Shipping Charges...	**Shipping**	_____
	Media Mail First Book ……..... $3.95 Each additional book………….$1.50	**Total**	$_____

(No Personal Checks Accepted)
Make Institutional Checks or Money Orders payable to:
New Vision Publication